The Next Chapter

Laura Muto

The Next Chapter

To my grandmothers, who are no longer here,
but continue to watch over me and love me
every day.

Part One

Chapter 1

Giovanna

"And how did that make you feel?"

I can't help but snicker at her- what a stupid question. I mean, what am I supposed to say? That I'm over the moon? That I'm doing great? No! I literally want to curl up in a ball and disappear into the never-ending bliss of nothingness.

I look down at my bouncing leg, unable to stop my nervous tick. "Horrible," I say.

"Horrible," Nancy repeats with a nod of her head, as if she knows exactly how I feel. "Anything else?"

Hold on. Why is she the one asking me questions? I'm paying her to tell me what to do- that's how therapy works, right? To be completely honest, I don't even want to be here. I'm only here because when I got home two weeks ago, my brother booked me for this appointment. I love Antonio, and I feel bad I left my family in the dust at the peak of my fame, so I'm here for him.

Make absolutely no mistake, I don't want to be here. I don't need therapy and to spend a little over $200 for one session, I just need my old life back. And by old life, I mean my life a couple of weeks ago. Before I lost the deal and lost my relationship and my lifelong friendships. I lost everything, and it's all my fault. It's safe to say that I've spent the past weeks wallowing in self-pity and a swimming pool full of liquor.

Is it called self-pity when you can't stand to look at your own reflection? No, I don't think self-pity is the right word, it's more like I'm completely repulsed with myself.
I take a long, hard look at Nancy, but I can't even read her face. I don't see any judgment, or sympathy, or really much of anything; she's as natural as my curls.

"I'm humiliated to show myself in public," I admit, darting my eyes to the ground.

She lets out a small sigh in the back of her throat and jots down some notes. "So, just to clarify, you lost your record deal?"

It sounds even worse when it comes from someone else's mouth. "Yep."

She puts a finger to her chin in thought. "I see how that would be tough."

Obviously. That's why I'm paying her so much money, isn't it? So, can she give me advice? "It is." I hate that I'm crying in front of her already, but I can't seem to stop the tears strolling down my warm cheeks.

She looks at her watch. "How did you lose the deal?"

"I missed the deadline for our next album."

She cocks her head to the side, taking more notes. "Luca and Tony didn't think to say anything to you when they saw you had no songs?" she asks.

Good, I'm glad I'm not crazy for thinking the exact same thing. I've spent the last two weeks looking at where things went wrong, and yet I cannot seem to answer the question she just asked.

"When they would ask to see the songs, I told them I was still working on them and that I didn't want them to see them yet. I would say that they weren't perfect and I just needed some more time with the lyrics. They seemed to believe that, and they pretty much left me alone before I had the chance to explode on them," I explain. Whether I'm trying to justify myself or them, I don't know.

There's an uncomfortable amount of silence in the room before she says, "I don't think it's fair of them to blame *everything* on you."

I give her a shrug. "But I think it is fair; I blame myself for everything."

She sets her notebook down on the coffee table in front of her chair and leans her elbows on her knees. She stares me directly in my eyes as she whispers, "Tell me a little more about that feeling, Giovanna."

"The boys could have pushed more, sure, but they did ask about the songs and I always brushed them off and snapped at them. Samantha could have been more on top of her clients, sure, but she was putting faith in that her famous artists would get their work done on time. Everyone was doing their job and trusting me to do mine and I let every single one of them down. I disappointed everyone."

She lets me compose myself for a moment before she questions further. "And may I ask why you didn't have any songs written?"

"I got busy," I reply, not wanting to elaborate any further. "I also felt so much pressure to write the next big album the world had seen, especially after *Livin'* received all the love that it did. I knew everyone loved that album- it was our most popular one- so they had expectations for the next one. I didn't want to release something that would flop and disappoint them, or come up short in the eyes of the media. Plus, I tend to write sad, sloppy lyrics that I put together at three in the morning, but Reen wasn't looking for that. It felt a little hard to write what other people wanted to hear, rather than what I wanted to truly write about."

"Interesting." She lets out a small breath. "If you could write about anything without worrying about what people are expecting you to write, what would it be?"

How bad I messed up my life. "I don't know."

That seems to be my go-to sentence now: *I don't know*. I think I've said it more in the last fourteen days than I have in my entire life. I am all out of answers. But how can I be out of answers if I never really had any answers in the first place?

Nancy gives me a sympathetic smile. "That's okay."

"I lost everything," I say, tears threatening in the corners of my eyes again. "It's all my fault." It sounds like I'm taking pity on myself, but that's not my intention. I'm angry at myself, not pitiful.

"Have you spoken to either Luca or Tony since you found out your contract collapsed?"

The contract didn't collapse by mere chance, I grabbed it with my own two hands and broke it in half like a twig.

"No," I say truthfully. "They made it clear that I should never reach out to them ever again." Flashbacks of that night come rushing back to me, sending chills down my spine. I shiver unexpectedly and Nancy writes something down. I'm sure she thinks that my reaction is some sort of sign, but there's really no reading her neutral expressions.

"I'm sure they didn't mean *ever*."

I shake my head. "Believe me, they want nothing to do with me and I can't say I blame them at all."

She gives me another sympathetic look, and I'm not sure how I feel about it. Am I supposed to be receiving any sympathy? I don't think I deserve any, but maybe Nancy is the only person who sees something in me that is still fixable.

She looks at her watch on her wrist again and sighs. "As our first session is coming to an end, I need to ask you one last question before we wrap this up."

I nod my head. "Sure."

"What's your goal by the end of our sessions? How do we want to feel and what do we need to achieve by talking to me?"

Well, considering that Antonio is the one who signed me up for these sessions, I'm not entirely sure. I don't want to tell her that I'm here because my brother forced me to, that will only hurt her feelings, and I don't want to do that. It's not that Nancy is a bad person; I just think that therapy is costing me nothing but money right now- money that I really don't have. However, if Antonio thinks this will help, then I'll do anything to get back into good grace with my family because I reek of desperation.

"I want to be content," I blurt, saying the only thing that came to my mind.

"How so?"

Again, with the questions. This whole session, she's basically been asking me questions and offering no advice. Maybe I should tell her I'm here to get advice and insight on what I should do with my life now, not receive questions and have to explain myself.

"When I was in Insieme, I was always looking to get more." I hate that I'm talking about Insieme in the past tense, as though it happened so long ago. It breaks my heart. "I was always looking to grow the fanbase, buy more products, release more songs, get on more billboards, and top the charts. I never really took a moment to stop and think about how good I was doing in the moment. I would look for the next best thing I could possibly come out with. I was never content with my life, so I want to be content once these sessions are over."

I've never admitted that out loud, but the fact that this is completely confidential makes me feel somewhat comfortable. It's been four years of being under contract, four years of not being able to say how I truly feel. It's a nice change, one I'm willing to stick with if it's what it takes to get my old life back.

I already miss waking up to Tony's phone shoved in my face because I'm wrapped around Luca, I miss talking to Kassie before heading onto stage, I miss going out on the streets and not getting asked what happened to Insieme. I miss the boys, I miss Luca, I miss Mary, and I miss touring. I miss how naive I was when I thought that everything was peaches and cream in Hollywood; I guess ignorance is truly bliss.

I take a deep breath before saying, "I also want to be able to look in the mirror and not feel completely sick to my stomach at the sight of my reflection."

Nancy's big eyes meet mine as she says, "I can help you, Giovanna."

Chapter 2

Luca

"I don't know what to do with myself," I say, throwing myself down on the couch next to Tony.

"Me, too. I still can't believe we're back here."

I look at him, wondering if he's thinking about Giovanna like I am- I wonder if he thinks about her as much as I do, but I don't think that's possible. She's the only thing I think about when I wake up, talk with my family, go to work, and she's the last thought I have when my head hits my pillow.

I firmly believe that you can love someone and still let them go. You can recognize when you're getting hurt and decide to leave the relationship, even if you still have so much love for that person.

I shake my head. "Samantha offered us that deal, but it doesn't seem right to take it without Gia." Don't get me wrong, working on the construction sites with my dad is absolutely brutal. It's hard, physical labor, and long hours. I would much rather be on tour singing my heart out than be waking up at 6:30 every morning to break cement.

But I won't take that deal Samantha gave us. She called Tony and I to tell us that Reen wanted Insieme to continue... just without Giovanna. Insieme would be known as a duo rather than a trio, and that seems wrong in my mind.

Tony nods his head, folding his arms behind his head and sinking further into the couch. "Insieme isn't Insieme without Giovanna, everyone knows that."

I agree. There would simply be no way Tony and I could get up on stage and still call ourselves Insieme without Gia being by our side. I miss her so much, but I'm still pissed at her.

"Maybe it's time we consider doing our own thing," Tony suggests weakly, but even as he says it, I know that solo careers won't happen. Sure, Tony and I make the music, but we still need lyrics. Without Giovanna's mastermind to come up with the most heartfelt lyrics the world has ever heard, our music doesn't serve any purpose. Yes, I am extremely upset with her for just throwing away our career, but there is no denying that she's talented.

Talented people need help sometimes too, you know, we aren't perfect.

I love her, and that's the reason I haven't reached out to her thus far. She has to be able to handle things on her own because I'm not always going to be there to baby her; I won't always be there to hold her hand.

"Tony, I miss her," I say, feeling completely comfortable enough to cry in front of my best friend. "I really did want to marry her. I'm worried for her, but I can't do anything."

He pats my shoulder. "I miss her too, buddy," he whispers, his words full of compassion.

Maybe I could have done something more to help her. I should have told her that I love her at least three times a day, so maybe I could have saved her from falling so far down. Do you know how hard it was to watch the love of my life fall further and further down as time went on? It broke my heart and tore me to pieces.

"I shouldn't have left her," I finally admit, saying the same thought that's been consuming me every night.

"She lost our contract," Tony points out.

I sit up. "That doesn't mean I've stopped loving her."

Tony straightens out his back, copying me. "Don't get me wrong, I still love her too. It's hard to wake up and not have her with us, but you would have done yourself and her a disservice if you stayed with her."

"But it would have been worth it!" I yell, getting mad at myself, not Tony. "I wanted to marry her, T, but nothing worked out like it was supposed to. Nobody could have predicted that we wouldn't have control over our own damn lives. If I love her so much, then why did I leave her and let her fend for herself?"

"Because she left us!" he cries. "She threw us away as if we were a piece of garbage. She was crying out for help, but when he tried to help her, she told us that she was fine or that she didn't want to talk about it. I know you feel guilty, hell, *I* feel guilty, but there was nothing more we could've done to save her. She truly brought this on herself."

I shake my head in disbelief at how messed up my life is. "I know, and it hurt me to watch her drink that much. I should have said something, rather than just talking to Mary about it."

Tony snickers to himself. "I don't really understand why Mary felt the need to ask you to keep an eye on her, because if she was so concerned, then she should have reached out to Gia herself."

My shoulders deflate. "She tried to reach out, but Gia turned her away. She got too busy with the tour, with the lifestyle. She forgot her roots."

Tony throws his arms up. "Exactly, she didn't want our help. She had so many supporters out there, yet she still felt alone because she turned everyone down. She was afraid to let her best friends in, so there must be something deeper there, especially with her drinking habits."

I look at Tony with tears in my eyes. "Do you think she's still drinking that much?"

He doesn't respond because the answer is painfully obvious. If she was drinking because she couldn't handle the stress of tour, we can only imagine how much she's been drinking since not being on tour. She must be going absolutely stupid, but we have no way of knowing.

She hasn't posted anything ever since I told her we couldn't get married. She used to love posting, and as our career took off, she started caring a little more about what she would post. She stopped looking at the comments for good so she wouldn't see all the hate comments.

I could always tell when she looked at those comments, though, because she would love this idea that Tony and I had come up with and she would look at us as if we were the smartest people to ever walk the earth. However, the next day she would see us and tell us that maybe we should reconsider because it "wasn't the right move", so of course I knew she looked at the comments. I wish she wouldn't have because I know how much they affect everyone. Back to our YouTube days, I would be so hurt over a single comment, so I decided to never look at the comments again for the sake of my mental health, and I've stuck to my word thus far.

"Have you seen the newest article on her?" Tony asks.

I know it's not a reliable source, but I would love to see a picture of her, I would love to see where she's at. I need *something* to fill this empty void in my lonely heart. "Show me."

Tony passes his phone to me and I gawk my eyes at the screen. I've always thought she was beautiful, *always*. She was never cocky about it though, and that made her ten times more attractive. She was confident, sure, but she was never flaunting herself around because she knew she was a looker. She was modest and real. She didn't want to give the paparazzi all that fake Botox they live for, she prided herself with staying natural.

But she looks terrible.

Her curls are still there, though they are knotted and unkept. Her eyes are sunk into the dark circles under her once passionate eyes. Is that her dad's shirt that she's wearing? I don't know, but I know the real Giovanna would never leave the house with a rip in an oversized shirt.

I give Tony his phone back quickly. "I can't read that, T. I just can't." My voice is barely a whisper. "I'm worried about her."

"Me too," he hushes, shutting off his phone and throwing it over his shoulder nonchalantly.

I am lost, there's no denying that. I don't know if I'll ever go back on tour, or if I'll ever be able to release another album again. All I know right now is that I am lost, but I have my best friend to walk down this windy, unknown path hand-in-hand with me. We're all in the same boat, and I know that Tony and I will row that boat as far as we possibly can, but I'm unsure if we'll be able to bring Giovanna to shore this time.

Chapter 3

Mary

I feel my phone buzz in my pocket as I'm showing my students what dance move comes next in the new dance I choreographed. Nowadays, no one is reaching out to me, so I know it must be important, so I tell the girls to take a water break. It still feels weird instructing without Giovanna, especially since all the students ask about her every class. She had an impact on these kids and everyone around her, and it's such a shame that she lost contact with everyone, particularly those who cared about her the most.

I open my phone and try my best to suppress the gasp that is trying to escape my lips. I don't know what I was expecting, but it wasn't a news alert notifying me that the "infamous Giovanna Rossi" was spotted coming out of a therapy session.

I knew she needed help, that's why I would always call her. Seeing as though she screened my calls and exploded on me when she found out Luca

and I were concerned about her drinking, I was not
expecting to see her in therapy.

She looks… *awful*. If it weren't for the
headline, I wouldn't have been able to recognize my
once best friend. Look, admitting to yourself that
you should probably be in therapy is a big step in
itself, so I'm proud of her for doing that. However,
knowing that pictures are most likely going to be
published of you walking out of a therapist's office
and still going to the appointment anyways takes
some real guts that not everyone has.

Let me make one thing crystal clear: I don't
want Giovanna to lose. Yes, I may have told her
that we should take some time apart, but that's only
because the friendship had become one-sided and
toxic. I don't think I should be worried when I'm
speaking on the phone to my best friend because
I'm scared, she might yell at me if I say the wrong
thing. And why would she yell at me? Because of
her fame. Yet she never once stopped and asked
herself how that made me feel- the fact that she
would constantly remind me that she'd moved on

up in life and I was still stuck in my same old routine. I'm still instructing the same girls who are years older now, I'm still living in the same city, buying the same clothes, and going to university getting myself a dead-end degree that will leave me with nothing but student debt. She was selling out stadiums having paparazzi following her around like an angry mob, and seeing that made me feel as though I had achieved nothing.

At first, I was naturally happy for her like any best friend would be. As time went on, however, she started to talk about herself and never asked how I was doing, barely letting me get two sentences in. I found that I couldn't sympathize with her for living the glamorous lifestyle she always wanted and had asked for.

But if she's in therapy now, maybe her life wasn't as perfect as I thought it was. Guilt starts to creep its way into my heart, as I start to think that maybe I shouldn't have just snapped at her and cut her off.

"Is everything okay, Miss Mary?" Eva asks, noticing how much time has passed and how silent I've been.

I will never admit to my kids that my heart is broken, and I also refuse to teach this class if I'm not giving them one hundred percent of my attention. It's not fair to the girls, so I decide we should end ten minutes early today. "You guys can pack up your stuff and I'll see you next week! We're ending a little early today because you have been working super hard and it's important to get some rest."

The girls are way more enthusiastic to go home and leave than I would have hoped, because I'm sure they would have loved to spend more time in class with Giovanna.

The girls quickly leave, and I'm even quicker to send them off, barely making sure they got to their cars okay. Once I head back into the studio, I'm overcome with an overwhelming sadness. My best friend isn't here anymore.

She's not here in this room with me, sipping her lemonade because she hates coffee. She's not here to make me laugh and tell me that everything is going to work out when I'm having a breakdown. The best part is that I'm the one who made her go and encouraged her to go because I wanted her to succeed.

I didn't know that the day I told her to go, would be the last day that I truly had my best friend. Having to end my friendship with her was like losing a sister. No, it wasn't *like* losing a sister, I *did* lose my sister. I lost the only person who taught me to have fun and let loose, and I don't think there will ever be a person in this world who can ever hold a candlestick to what she was.

I stare at her name in my contacts, trying to mourn a person who is very much still alive, wondering if my pride or heart is going to win this time and if I'll ever reach out again.

Chapter 4

Giovanna

I'm not even surprised that my phone is drier than a desert after the articles came out about me. I'm glad, though, because I didn't want people reaching out to me and having awkward conversations. I should have known better to wear a hoodie and a ball cap so no one would have been able to recognize me. The boys and I used to do that all the time when we would go out, but I just don't feel famous anymore, so I didn't even give it a second thought.

I used to be on top of the world, soaring so high that I was above cloud nine. Being up that high with so many eyes watching me, I had people telling me what to do and controlling my actions. Now that Reen won't touch me with a ten-foot pole, I have no one to tell me how to act.

I should have known that what Reen was offering was way too good to be true. I should have done more research, and maybe not have signed right away. I mean, what kind of normal person would come across Insieme's page and automatically offer them a deal? At the time, I thought it was that simple and that it was our golden ticket to fame, and in some ways, it was. I know now that Reen is anything but normal.

"Ignorance is bliss," I mutter under my breath as I make my way to the fridge. I'm staying in a motel because, really, what other choice do I have? I don't blame my family for not welcoming me back with open arms, especially after I ghosted them after winning a Grammy. They didn't completely disown me, but they're tired of me constantly running back to them and then leaving them; they're sick of putting up with my crap.

I reach for the six pack of beer I bought, which wouldn't be my first choice, but it's the cheapest so here we are.

I crack one open and take a big swig as I open my phone. I scroll past the hundreds of comment notifications, moving my finger as fast as possible so I don't have to read them. I haven't posted anything on social media in months, so fans think the way to reach out to me is to comment on my old posts. From what catches my eye, a lot of them say they miss me and they hope I'm doing okay.

I am not doing okay, and I haven't been for a while.

I take another drink and feel pure adrenaline rush into my veins. The substances I'm putting into my body make me open my contacts and scroll to the only person I want to talk to right now. I'm almost certain he won't pick up, but I hit his number anyway.

To my surprise, he picks up on the first ring. "Hello?"

I can't tell if he's asking his greeting because he doesn't know why I'm calling, or if he doesn't know *who* is calling because he probably deleted my number.

"Hey, it's Giovanna."

"I know."

I shut my eyes; he has every right to give me the cold shoulder. Now that he's picked up, I'm not even sure why I called him in the first place. "Luca, I'm so sorry-"

"Stop," he whispers, clipping my pathetic apology right away. "Why are you calling me?"

Again, I don't have an answer for him. I wasn't expecting him to jump right back into a relationship with me if he picked up, but I've never heard Luca be this short before.

I didn't know it only took two weeks for someone to fall completely out of love. If Luca can move on, why can't I?

Now I just feel stupid, knowing that I think about him every second of every passing day, and he wants nothing to do with me. There was still a part of me that thought Luca would come around. I mean, we're Luca and Gia- the cutest couple in Hollywood.

Looking back, my thought process was stupid. We're not in Hollywood, we're never getting back together, and he doesn't love me anymore. He *hates* me.

"I'm not sure," I say truthfully, stupidly.

He sighs with clear annoyance. "Giovanna."

I just miss his voice, and I need to know if he misses me too. All too often, friendships or relationships fall completely apart because they aren't able to communicate with one another. Or one person thinks the other person is mad at them, and then the relationship collapses right beneath them.

I have my answers now. I can hear it in his voice- his tone- that all we are now are simply strangers with a few memories now.

"Luca."

"What do you need?"

I need you. "Nothing, I guess."

"Sure."

There's a long, awkward pause between us. I've wanted to talk to him for two weeks, imagining exactly how our conversation would go once I got him on the phone so I could apologize. Yet I'm completely frozen. It's so silent between us that you could hear a pin drop, until he goes, "Have you been drinking?"

"No," I lie through my teeth. I know he doesn't believe me because he lets out a snort on the other line and it makes my heart drop that he already knew I was drinking.

"I really have to go, Giovanna," he says pathetically, sounding as done with this horrible conversation as he possibly could.

"I miss you," I blurt out, knowing that if I didn't get that off my chest, I would regret it for the rest of my life. "I miss you, Luca."

"You can come over tonight then because this doesn't feel like an appropriate conversation to have over the phone." He sounds cold, but it's something. "I'll send you my address."

Before I can even make an excuse not to go, Luca hangs up and texts me his address within seconds. My heart was already pounding from adrenaline, alcohol, and Luca, but now? Now it's kicked into full overdrive.

Chapter 5

Luca

I don't know what I was thinking, inviting her over here. I wouldn't dare tell Tony, I'm just glad he's working at a restaurant so he's gone almost every night. Tony and I are sharing this small flat, barely making rent, so he claims that he works six days a week at Milestones because our rent is due soon. But I know my best friend and I know that he's just working to take his mind off of everything. Work is a good distraction for him.

If he's not working, he's thinking, and that's scary right now. Yes, the media may have spread rumors about us, but they got Tony right- he oozes out love. Love radiates off him like the sun on a scolding hot summer day. He will love anyone no matter who they are with his whole heart; he wears his vulnerable heart on his sleeve. And when you break his trust, you hurt him.

Giovanna hurt my best friend really bad, and she hurt me. Tony is fuming right now, and I can't say that I blame him. Not only is he dealing with the loss of our record deal, but he's mourning his ex-best friend. Mourning someone who is still alive is incredibly painful and he's going through that right now, so extra shifts for him keep him sane.

As I hear the doorbell ring, I'm grateful Tony isn't here. It feels sort of like a betrayal, going behind his back and inviting her to our flat when he specifically told me he wants nothing to do with her now.

But I can't help it, and she really didn't give me a choice. I need to see the woman I still love, and the conversation she wants to have should not happen over the phone. I know that by the end of this visit, I'll either want to extend a hand and pull Gia back on her feet, or I'll walk away from her forever. Which one, I don't know yet, all I can do is open the door and pray for the best.

I thought that maybe the photos in the articles were making her look worse than she is in person, but I'm sorry to say that they were spot on.

"Come on in," I say, trying to hide my discomfort and stop staring. It's hard though because so much has changed in the last couple of weeks.

She nods her head as she walks in, and it's awkward to say the least. I can't make idle chit-chat, I am *definitely* not offering her a drink, and the fact that she's examining my carpet with such intensity is a clear sign that she doesn't know what she's doing here either. Time for me to break the ice, like I always have to do when we're fighting.

I clear my throat, snapping us out of complete silence. "We need to talk."

"Yeah," she says meekly, following me to the family room and sitting on a chair opposite of me. I sink into the sofa and wait for her to say something. Anything. She's the one who said she missed me, so there is no way I'm going to start this conversation.

"How have you been?" she finally asks.

I scrunch my eyebrows at this, trying to keep my cool. My father always tells me I inherited my grandfather's anger issues and he is right on the money with that one. I'm working on it.

She rolls her lips together and nods her head as if she's disappointed with my lack of response. And my parent's advice of trying to stay calm goes right out the front door. "I don't know what you're expecting me to say?"

"Nothing," she says with a shrug.

"Nothing?" I coax my eyebrows up. "Then why the hell did you call me?" I feel my anger boiling higher and higher like a raging tea kettle, and I'm not sure how much longer I can go without reaching my boiling point.

"Because I miss you."

I shake my head and give a cold laugh. "I can't believe you sometimes, you know that? How *dare* you call me out of the blue, not saying anything, and then tell me you *miss* me. Giovanna, you're the reason we don't talk anymore, you're the reason we're not on tour, and you're the reason my life is ruined." I can feel my veins popping out of my neck as I yell, but I'm unable to stop my emotions from bubbling over.

"Luca, please, just-"

"No! Has it ever occurred to you that maybe you owe Tony and I an apology?"

Her lips quiver, and for a split second, I feel a pang of guilt. I start to think that maybe I should let up a bit, but then she says something that makes me see red.

"And you should be apologizing to me as well, but here we are."

"Are you serious right now? Are you genuinely serious?"

She folds her arms. "I'm not saying that I didn't do anything wrong, but what I am saying is that we all did things we shouldn't have. I don't think we should get into what would have or should have happened because we can't change the past. I've done things, you've done things, and Tony has done things that we all know damn well were not for the greater good of Insieme."

"There is no more Insieme anymore because of you! I can't believe you're trying to turn this on us right now, Giovanna." The fact that Tony isn't here makes me want to defend him even more because Giovanna is way out of line right now.

"But think about our past, Luca. We used to be head over heels for each other. I still love you, Luca. Every day I wake up, and I reach out for you, but then I'm hit with this painful blast of coldness because you're not there; I'm alone. I miss laughing with you, kissing you, and being myself around you, and the fact that I don't have you anymore has created this void in my heart that will never be filled."

It breaks my heart to say it, but I know it has to be said for both of us. "There is no us anymore."

A tear streams down her cheek, and I can't tell if I want to give her the biggest hug or throw her out of my flat.

I end up choosing the latter.

"I think you should get going now," I whisper harshly.

She shoots her head down. "I am sorry, Luca, you have to know that."

But how do I know that, exactly? She's doing what she always does- she's putting the blame on everyone else but herself, and I'm quite honestly sick of it.

I can't keep forgiving her without holding her accountable. It's not fair to me, and it's not fair to her, I'm making the decision to let her go.

Chapter 6

Tony

I am completely exhausted when I get home from work. I've spent six hours running back and forth across the entire restaurant without a break. Here's the thing about the restaurant business: you don't get any breaks. Ever. Drinking water? Forget it.

But I love my job. I've found a second family in a short amount of time. I wholeheartedly believe that you meet some of the coolest people when working at a restaurant. They were the friends I didn't know I needed.

So as soon as I get home and Luca goes, "I need to tell you something," I just know it has something to do with Giovanna. The fact that I've found new friends and have started to move on with my life, yet I still need to deal with her nonsense, boils my blood.

"I can't believe this," I say, shaking my head. If I still had any energy left in me, I would be pacing the room like I always am, but I'm so tired of *everything*.

"I shouldn't have invited her over, and I'm sorry," Luca apologizes.

I rub my eyes and let out a loud sigh. "Yeah, you shouldn't have." He looks at me with worried eyes. "I'm not mad at you," I clarify. "She wasn't able to hold herself accountable when Insieme was together, and she clearly hasn't changed. Why didn't you tell me she was coming over?" Luca shouldn't have had to deal with her all by himself.

He shrugs his shoulders as if it isn't a big deal. "I knew you would be completely opposed to having her step foot into our flat. Plus, you were working."

"Valid," I state with a stoic expression.

"And I knew that things would have gotten even more heated if you were here," he continues.

I don't even take offense to Luca's comment. Perhaps it's because I'm too tired, or perhaps I don't have anything to defend because I know he is right. "Luca, I really don't want to give her a second chance."

At this, he stands up from his spot and sits directly next to me. "T, I'm hurt too. She destroyed us. I mean, look at us! We had the whole world behind us and it all fell down. Now I'm working long mornings on construction sites and you're busting your ass at a restaurant and you might not even get tips on some tables."

"Don't even get me started on the non-tippers," I say, turning my nose up. Seriously, don't get me started on how disrespectful and privileged they are.

"And it's all because of her, and I know that. We should have dropped another album and been on tour right now, and we could have probably won another Grammy, I bet you."

I look into his eyes, which are rimmed with black circles. He's looked exhausted ever since Insieme's break, but I can't imagine I look any better myself.

"I know, Luca, so I'm telling you that we have to let her go. We gave her one too many chances."

I know I'm being harsh, but I'm not even speaking my full truth. I really want to tell him that I wish Giovanna would have just kept her damn mouth shut and not told us about her dream. If I could go back in time, I would go and scream at my 16-year-old self to not go to Lane's because his life would get ruined if he did. I'm mad at myself that I just jumped head first into her mastermind of a plan without questioning why. Why are we doing this? What happens when it doesn't work out? Why me and Luca?

As much as Giovanna got blinded by the glamor, I was blinded at the beginning too. I chose not to finish high school and to follow Giovanna to Hollywood. I chose to drop out because once I do something, I need to put my full attention into it. I didn't want to be distracted if I was going to be making music in Hollywood, but I know that I was wrong back then. We simply weren't ready.

Luca turns his head towards me and looks at me with sympathy in his eyes. "Why are you more upset at her than I am?"

"I might now have dated her, but she still kicked me when I was down," I snap. I might not have kissed her in front of thousands of screaming fans and flashing cameras, but we still had a bond that I don't think I'll be able to find with anyone else.

"Let me put it to you this way, Luca," I say, trying not to hurt his feelings because I'm not upset with him. I'm mad at Giovanna and I'm trying not to take it out on him. "How many people have I come out to?"

Silence. He doesn't need to answer, and he won't answer because he knows exactly where I'm going with this.

"Only you and Giovanna knew. I trusted you guys because I felt safe with you. You were the first people to ever make me feel like it was okay to just be myself. It was a secret that I had been keeping for a long time- my whole life, to be exact- so obviously our friendship meant something to me. It didn't mean anything to her and she threw it all away as if it were nothing."

He pursues his lips together as he pinches the bridge of his nose. I hate that we're giving Giovanna this much time and energy still because she isn't worth the waste of breath.

"I love you, T. You've been my best friend since birth, and I can't imagine my life without you. I'm sorry if I ever made you feel like your feelings were little or ignored you. What do you mean she kicked you when you were down, though? I don't understand," he says, leaning forward as he waits for my answer.

I kick myself internally. I shouldn't have let that comment slip because I'm not ready to tell anyone- not even Luca- what I meant by it. I can hardly understand it myself, so if I can't grasp the situation myself, how could I possibly explain it to others?

Instead of elaborating, I choose to deflect with humor like I always do. "Here we go again with the 'I love you' speeches. Honestly, never stay up past midnight because you're always dropping the 'L' word like it's going out of style," I laugh.

Luca turns his head to the side and opens his mouth, clearly confused in my mood change, but I need a way out of this conversation. There is no way I'm going to tell Luca what I've been dealing with, because once I start, I won't be able to stop.

You know when something terrible happens to you and you're suddenly overwhelmed with emotions? Well, that's what happened to me. It happened when I was still in Insieme, but it was easy not to think about my pain because I was on tour and distracted.

The tour ended, though.

When Insieme broke up, I was left drowning in an ocean full of depressing emotions. Being alone is scary because that means there is no one there to keep your mind occupied. Those thoughts just keep rushing and rushing and the pain keeps coming and coming. But for me, it never ends. The pain never stops; it consumes my whole body.

I think what complicates my feelings the
most is that I can't communicate what exactly went
down because I'm still trying to figure it all out
myself. It feels like I've been trying to figure myself
out my whole life, as if something is wrong with
me, and I'm burnt out.

"I have to work a double shift tomorrow, so
I should get some sleep. Goodnight, Luca." I get up
and start to walk to my bedroom, ignoring Luca
who is calling after me because I can't and won't
open up to anyone about why the last two years in
Insieme were the lowest point of my life.

I guess it's hard for me to speak up because
I've been silent my whole life.

Chapter 7

Giovanna

I can't stop crying and I hate it. I hate that Nancy has to see me cry, even though I know she deals with sobbing clients regularly.

"It's okay," Nancy says, "let it all out."

So, I do. I tell her everything that happened last night. I explain how Luca wants nothing to do with me, how I got yelled at by someone who used to love me, and just how utterly stupid and alone I feel.

Once I've got it all out of my system, I feel lighter. Weightless.

"What made you call Luca in the first place?" Nancy asks.

"Well, obviously, I miss him," I say as if she should already know this. Again, I respect Nancy, but why is it always *her* asking *me* questions?

She lets out a chuckle. "I know you miss him very much, but what made you pick up the phone and talk to him?"

My mouth moves faster than my brain as I say, "I had been drinking, and…" I trail off. I should not have said that. Nancy will not let this one go; I just know it. "And I let my emotions get the best of me," I finish.

You know what I hate? Silence. I can't stand it, in fact. I find it extremely uncomfortable and unnerving.

"Hm, that's interesting," Nancy whispers to herself. "How often do you drink?"

Everyday.

"Occasionally."

She shoots her eyebrows up. "This is interesting. I feel like we're getting somewhere, so let's stay here for a while."

No.

"Okay, so you drink occasionally." She pauses as if she's waiting for me to respond and confirm that.

I swallow the lump in my throat. "Yep."

She nods. "And when did you first start really drinking?"

"16."

She writes something down quickly in her notes. "Okay, and how do you feel when you're drinking?"

I shrug. "I'm not sure I understand your question." I do understand, though, because I can feel my heart pounding against my rib cage.

"Sorry, I should be more specific. Do you drink with others?"

"I used to," I say truthfully, "but I don't really have anyone to go out with now."

"So, you drink alone," she says matter-of-factly. I can't understand her tone nor can I read her facial expression, as usual.

"I guess."

"And I'm guessing it isn't for fun?"

"Excuse me?"

She locks eyes with me and I can't seem to peel my gaze away from her. I know she's got me right where she wants me, and I feel worried. I feel a sudden wave of heat come over me and my hands feel clammy.

"How much did you have to drink before you called Luca?" she asks.

I flare out my nostrils. "What are you trying to say right now, Nancy?"

She puts her notebook down. "I'm not trying to say anything," she clarifies. "I'm just trying to understand you, so I can help you as much as possible."

"Well, stop! I'm telling you that you're beating down the wrong bush. I know exactly what you're trying to squeeze out of me, and it won't work." I fold my arms on my stomach, trying to calm down my racing heartbeat. All of a sudden, it feels like walls are caving in on me and Nancy's office is the size of a Smurf's house.

"You're angry." Do all therapists point out the obvious? "I can tell I've struck a nerve, so why don't I just ask some yes or no questions to keep things to a minimum. I don't want to upset you." It's not like I can tell her how to do her job, so I have no choice but to nod my head.

"Did you drink when you were in Insieme?"

"Yes."

"Did you go out drinking with Tony and Luca?"

"Yes."

"Were they the ones who initiated going out?"

"No."

"Were you the only one who wanted to go out?"

"No."

"How many drinks does it take for you to start feeling a buzz?"

I think about this. "That's not a yes or no question," I point out. She squints her eyes at me and lets out a small laugh. "Around four or five."

She nods her head. "Have you ever tried to stop drinking and failed?"

"No, I've never tried to stop."

She nods her head again as she purses her lips. "Has your drinking affected your life at home?"

I think about what my "home" is now. It was the boys, and my family, of course. When I was on the road, my home was Insieme, but now? I'm staying in a motel, and I'm so close yet so far from my original home.

"Yes." I start crying again. "I don't want to answer any more questions, please."

"Giovanna, I think we found something here, and I'm going to do my very best to make sure you get the help you need. I'm not giving you a diagnosis, but I'm starting to get a better idea of you and how to help you. As hallmark as it may sound, you are not alone in this. There are plenty of organizations out there that are willing to help you get through this. I can't help you if you don't want to be helped, though, so I have one last question. Do you want my help, Giovanna?"

I blink at her several times. "Are you saying that I'm an…" The word gets stuck in a lump in my throat.

"I don't want to jump to any conclusions, Giovanna, but I do have some homework for you," she clarifies. "I want you to go home and reflect on my questions that I asked you. I also want you to think about your reaction- were you mad? Were you annoyed? Why were you feeling that way? I want you to reflect on our session when you leave and come with answers to your next appointment."

I look at her through my teared vision. "Yes." I sound exasperated, exactly how I feel.

She cocks her head to the side. "Yes?"

My lips are dry and chapped as I speak. "I want your help."

"I'm over the moon to hear," she says with a smile.

I've faced many twists and turns in my life, walking down different paths. I didn't choose the right ones most of the time, I'm sure everyone in my life can see that. I'm confident in one thing, though: this is a step in the right direction for once in my life, and I'm glad Nancy is there to be my safety net, ready to catch me if I fall further.

Chapter 8

Luca

I've been thinking a lot lately. For days, my mind has been elsewhere, as if I'm not here, disconnected. My dad's favorite thing to do now is to yell at me on the job site because I've "got my head up my ass", and I just give him a small laugh because I don't want to tell him that I'm miserable here.

I don't want all the back-breaking work, the long hours, and the excruciating pain I put my body through. I don't want to hear Vince rub it in my face that he was right. Do normal brothers pray for each other's downfall? No, but nothing about the Fonzo family is normal.

Vince and I went head-to-head for so long, and when I found out we were losing the deal, I told Giovanna I should have listened to Vince. The truth is, though, is that I hate his guts. I hate that I've been in his shadow my whole life, and when I was in Insieme, I was finally my own person. I was no longer in his shadow, and my ego allowed me to enjoy every damn second of it.

When I moved back from Los Angeles, I was disgusted that Vince had an evil smirk plastered onto his face, as if he was thrilled to see me lose everything. He didn't even bother nor cared to ask how I was doing, and everyone could see I was at my lowest. And I haven't made much progress.

You know those inspirational quotes you see on social media about how life always gets better? Well, when is it my turn? How long do I have to suffer until this life of mine turns around for the better? It's not like I'm sitting at home moping around.

Okay, that is exactly what I'm doing right now, but this is rare. I just got home from an eleven-hour shift, so I think I've earned the right to sit and let my emotions flow, instead of suppressing them.

I stare at Samantha's name in my contacts, wondering where she's been. The person who was supposed to have our "best interest" has disappeared off the face of the earth. Once all of the paperwork was settled, she didn't want to talk to us again. I can't say I blame her, but she was a bad manager if you ask me.

Yes, I miss Giovanna and it tore me apart to kick her out of my flat, but the fact of the matter is that I have to put my feelings for her aside right now. I've seen the pictures, the articles, and even in real life. She is terrible, and Tony and I aren't that much ahead of her.

When we were together, Giovanna would always tell me that I'm her rock, holding her down. I think she was wrong and that it was never me. The rock was Insieme, it kept us all grounded. Insieme was the foundation of our lives, and we all came crumbling down as soon as there was a crack in it.

Insieme brought us together years ago, and I truly believe it'll bring us back again.

I call Samantha's number.

"Samantha speaking." She picks up on the first ring.

"Hello, it's-"

"Luca Fonzo. What can I do for you?" At first it sounds like she's annoyed and can't wait to get off the phone, but then I remember how she used to go a thousand miles a minute and I shouldn't take it personally.

"Is now a good time to talk?" I ask.

"Depends on what you want to talk about," she states bluntly.

"I had an idea, and before you can shut it down, I want you to hear me out first," I reply quickly, trying to get everything off my chest before she hangs up on me.

"Okay, I'm sitting now. You have my full attention."

I let out a small breath, hyping myself up to pitch this glorious idea to my former manager. "Insieme needs to get back together," I blurt out.

She scoffs on the other line. "Are you crazy?"

"Maybe," I say, "but you know it would be a good move. Think about it- it will break the charts and top the headlines of every news press. Fans are waiting for us to drop an album, so that's what we need to do. There are various rumors swirling around as to why Insieme broke up, and none of us have addressed the public due to the contracts we signed. Fans are wanting us back, so Reen needs to take us back for things to go back to normal."

"I'm not convinced," she grumbles.

"Look, I haven't talked to Tony or Giovanna about this, but I really think we can pull together for one more merry go round to do this properly."

"Are you even hearing what is coming out of your mouth?" she asks. "First of all, Gia is too much of a liability- there are several rumors about her drinking habits, and Reen would be stupid to ruin our brand name and take her back."

I sit up taller as if she can see me. "What if I told you that I can get her sober?"

There's a silent pause on her end, and then she goes, "What?"

"You don't have to sign us right away, but you would be stupid to cut ties with us forever. You know how special and talented we are, I don't need to tell you that or sell our story to you. Yes, Giovanna messed up big time, but I need Insieme back in my life, and it's a good business move. I'll talk to Tony and he'll be on board with this."

She laughs at me. "On board with what, exactly? Because I've yet to give you an offer and I've already told you that we can't help you."

"You can't help us if Giovanna is still like this, but I believe she's going to change. I spoke with her the other day."

"You can't make a sculpture out of a broken piece of marble."

It truly makes me mad that Samantha still talks down towards Giovanna. I still love Gia, I'm just too mad at her right now to tell her that. But actions speak louder than words, right? Am I not proving that I still love her by trying to get a contract? When I tell her about this, she's bound to get sober; she'd be stupid not to.

"She just needs help, and that's something that you never cared to offer her. Sure, Gia ruined her own life, but you played a huge role in her downfall, Samantha. You tried to control all of our lives, especially hers by saying we couldn't get engaged and all. I will not have any of it this time; we will not take that from you anymore. If and when you sign us back, we expect to be treated with respect and like actual human beings."

"How are you so confident that Reen will accept you back with open arms?" she presses.

I shake my head because it's painfully obvious to me. "Because they'd be idiots not to, you and I both know that."

For once, she takes a second to think before she speaks. "I guess I do miss having you guys keep me on my toes."

Sometimes, less is more, so I choose not to say anything. I'm certain that I'm reeling in Samantha like a fish. I've got her hooked, lined, and-

"I'll have to talk to Reen, but keep your phone near you. Make no mistake, this isn't anything concrete, especially if Giovanna doesn't get her act together."

Sinker.

"Thank you, Samantha, truly." It feels wrong to thank the woman who ruined my chances of getting engaged. Perhaps it's wrong that I've even been on the phone with her, but I can see how much better off everyone was with Insieme than we are without. What other option do I have?

"I'll keep you updated as best as I can, but I'm telling you right now that you better be able to prove Giovanna has changed before we sign you again," she reiterates.

"On it."

We say our goodbyes and hang up, and I'm hit with a sudden sense of relief. For weeks I've felt nothing but bitterness and emptiness, but now there's finally something I can work for. I'm striving for a goal, rather than just getting up and going to work every day. I need to achieve my goal; I'm motivated.

My first course of action is to call Giovanna and club her in the head with the truth.

Chapter 9

Giovanna

I'm out for a walk and trying to do Nancy's homework, when I see an incoming call from Luca. Nancy suggested going out for daily walks, something about how it's been proven to boost your mental health, so I decided to give it a shot. I remember how much I used to love exercising before I was forced to train every single day, and how I would go run around my block. So, I wasn't as opposed to walking as I was to some of the other things Nancy suggested.

My first thought when Luca's name shows up on my screen is that someone must have died. Because, really, why else would he be calling after making it crystal clear he wants me out of his life for good?

"What's wrong?" I question as soon as I pick up his call.

"Nothing." I think I hear him let out a genuine chuckle, but I'm not one hundred percent sure. "I need to talk to you and I was wondering if I could take you out for dinner tonight?"

The way he says it and his tone sends shivers down my spine. I can't tell if they're good or bad shivers yet, but all I know is that this is the chance I needed to redeem myself.

"When and where?"

And that's how I ended up here, sitting across from my ex-boyfriend. I feel silly, sitting across from him in this low-dimmed family restaurant because I know I'm staring. I just can't keep my eyes off of him when he looks *this* handsome, though.

He's wearing black on black, something that would make any other person look odd and pale, but fits him like a glove. Luca has put on quite a bit of muscle since working with his dad. I know where he works because I've been checking his Instagram constantly, where he's always promoting his father's business and showing his followers the job sites. He looks amazing and I'm quite literally stunned to silence by his beauty.

Sitting across from him now, with a burger in front of me and a pizza in front of him, I know that I want him back in my life.

"I want to apologize for how I acted the other day. I was out of line, and I'm sorry," I say sheepishly, unsure of how he's going to take that. Another thing Nancy and I are working on is admitting when I'm wrong and to not point my finger at someone. It doesn't feel good by any means, but I know I need to do it in order to get the boys back into my life.

"I appreciate that, thank you," he says.

I flash him a genuine smile that shows all of my teeth, something I haven't done in a while. He seems relaxed tonight, so I take that as a good sign.

"Gia, I have to talk to you." As he says this, the waiter comes to see how our first few bites are. We assure him that it's fantastic and when he leaves me, my heart starts pumping. "What's up?" I try to play it cool, but I'm sweating buckets right now, and he knows it.

"I called Samantha."

Absolutely not. Luca and I are not together by any means, but I feel betrayed. My heart has sunk to my feet- how could he do this to himself, let alone me? Why would he even consider speaking to that *awful* woman? Does he not remember all the crap she put us through? It makes him just as bad of a person as Samantha to even consider reaching out. I would rather cut off all my arms and legs before I ever see or hear from Samantha again.

"I know you're upset." Even a toddler would be able to tell that I'm livid; I'm practically turning purple. "I was, and still am, upset at Reen as well. However, we have to be rational about this, Gia."

"Rational? Explain this to me, Luca, because I'm having a hard time understanding this."

And so, he tells me everything. I sit and stare at him, nodding a couple of times and acting like I'm still listening to him. I know that he wants Insieme to get back together, but I'm still waiting for him to explain why he thinks it's a good idea to go back to Reen.

"Does that make sense?" he asks once he's finished his little spiel. The waiter comes back to clear our plates and hands us a dessert menu.

"No," I whisper, shaking my head once the waiter is gone again.

It's not that I don't understand where he's coming from, because I do. I think the whole world knows by now that Insieme is much better together than we are apart, considering all three of us have fallen off the face of the earth music wise. The only content they get now are pictures from the paparazzi, and so far, two people have asked for our autographs at this restaurant.

He reaches for my hand across the table and grazes his thumb along my palm. I can feel my cheeks go as red as a lobster. "Gia, I made it clear to Samantha that we will not sign if she continues her toxic ways."

Despite how warm I feel inside with Luca's hand in mine, I snap back to reality. "People don't just change overnight, Luca. We should have never signed with them in the first place, and I won't make the same mistake twice."

He tilts his head, but doesn't remove his hand from mine. "You can say what you want about Samantha, but we would still be drinking beers and singing out of a dingy karaoke machine if it weren't for her, so she's not all that bad."

"She wouldn't let us get married!" I snap, yanking my hand out of his grip. I can't believe what I'm hearing. What doesn't he understand? Why can't he see that going back to Reen would hurt me even more?

He inhales a sharp breath, clearly hurt by my reaction. "I know, *amore*, I know."

"I don't know what you want me to say," I mumble.

"Well, nothing is for certain. We won't have a solid contract until-" He stops abruptly, as if he's been caught red-handed in a lie.

"Until what?" I press, my leg bouncing uncontrollably.

He clears his throat and casts his eyes downwards. "Until you get sober."

My previous session with Nancy flashes before my mind, and I realize I haven't had time to properly process it. Am I ready to admit that I need help, let alone admit to Luca that I may need serious help? The task seems all so daunting to me.

How do I get sober, exactly, if I want to get sober? I don't know how the rest of my life will pan out if I were to put down the bottle, and it's scary.

Here's the thing with me: everyone leaves. My family, though they had good reason to, left me. Luca, Tony, Samantha, Mary, and everyone else who I was close with, they all left. They told me they would be there for me at my lowest, and they were nowhere to be found because they were blowing in the wind. But you know what has never left me? Alcohol.

It kept me warm on my coldest nights and kept me afloat when I was drowning.

I just can't believe Luca really thought it would be a good idea to lay all of this out and put even more pressure on me to get sober. At the end of the day, it's my life and I only have to satisfy myself.

I don't have to get sober for Samantha, for Reen, or even for Luca. I can understand- and maybe even appreciate- where he's coming from, and I'm almost certain that it wasn't his idea to get a contract on the condition that I get sober. It was probably that evil witch Samantha, but Luca is entertaining it.

That's what hurts me the most. Not the fact that everyone thinks I'm an alcoholic and thinks I can't get my life together, because they aren't truly wrong, but Luca thinking this is a good idea is what hurts me the most. It also makes me lose some respect for him because I don't see how he could possibly think it's okay to approach me like this.

"Oh," I whisper, clenching down on my jaw.

I just wish I could come to the decision of getting sober on my own. I should be allowed time to reflect and make this decision on my own, and I don't think I deserve to be pressured like this by anyone.

"Giovanna, please, I've begged you before and I'm begging you again," he hushes, his voice cracking as he speaks.

"Just stop." I put a hand up to silence him. "I know that you think I need to stop drinking. In fact, I agree with you. Of course, you know that I see a therapist, I'm sure you've seen the articles. However, do you know what Nancy and I have been talking about recently? My drinking. She doesn't call it a problem like everyone else, nor does she make me feel like a monster, and I think that's why I'm so open to talking about it with her. She wanted me to go home and come to terms with what was discussed at the session; she allowed me to do that on my own terms.

"I can't stop drinking with a snap of my fingers. I can't just pretend like I don't depend on it as my only source of happiness and be miserable for the rest of my life. I don't think it's fair for anyone to ask me to get sober so we can go on tour again. It's a little bit selfish."

"I know, but, Giovanna, we can make Insieme work properly this time," he counters, looking at me with pleading eyes.

"I wasn't done," I say, cutting him off because I know that if I stop now, I will never be able to say this again. "I know that I hurt a lot of people, but I don't even understand my own situation right now. All I know is that I need to get better. However, if you think for one minute that I'm going to sit down in some random Alcoholic Anonymous meeting with a blue book in my hand because someone is requiring me to, you are sorely mistaken. I'm done meeting Reen's requirements, okay? I know I lost the deal, but at least she isn't putting unreasonable demands on me twenty-four-seven. So no, Luca, you can go tell her to blow that fake offer up her-"

"What about me, Giovanna?" Luca yells, slamming his hand down on the table. I'm certain every head in the restaurant has turned to us, and I hate the feeling of so many eyes on me right now.

"What about you? I said that I recognize I have an issue, so why can't you see that as a step in the right direction? I know I hurt you, and I'm so sorry."

"You're only apologizing because I told you to, though. As far as I'm concerned, you're giving me the lip service you think I want to hear your sorry excuse for an apology."

I shrug my shoulders because I'm at a loss. "That's not what happened at all."

"You're going to look at me right now and tell me you didn't try and push the blame onto Tony and I?" he asks, leaning forward so I can see the rage in his eyes.

"I don't know what else I can say to you to convince you that my intentions are genuine. I'm saying that I agree that Insieme should get back together at some point, but I'm certain we should not go back to Reen."

He scoffs under his breath, showing me that he's not satisfied with my answer at all. "What other options do we have?"

"Look, I know it may not seem like it, but I'm trying my best here. I really am. I just need a little bit more time to comprehend what I did and how I need to fix myself, and I don't need to be put on a timeline by anyone for that."

He laughs at me. "When have you ever cared about timelines, Giovanna?"

My heart drops to the floor at that comment, making me instantly nauseous. "I just need to clear my head and figure my life out before I jump back into Insieme," I whisper, my voice croaky as I wave the server over and ask for the bill. I know I disappointed Luca and didn't give him whatever answer he was looking for, so the least I can do is pay for his dinner.

I pick up the check as soon as it drops and make sure to leave a good tip. My pride chooses to ignore the cry my wallet makes as I tap my card and the waiter tells us to have a nice night. This dinner has made me rethink my choice of staying unemployed.

I roll my lips into each other as I look at Luca again. "I'm sorry, but just please try to understand where I'm coming from." I get up to leave, but what he says next stops me in my tracks.

"I'm proud of you."

"For what?" I ask, scrunching my eyebrows together because just one minute ago he was screaming at me.

"For seeing your drinking problem."

I smile to myself as I turn around to walk out the door. "I'll see you around, Luca."

I grab my purse and walk out feeling significantly lighter. I don't know what my future holds, but I'm glad I got it off my chest that I don't want to ever breathe the same air as Samantha. Hopefully, Luca can start to understand that, but what I gained from tonight is the fact that Luca can see how I'm not always the bad guy.

Sometimes a bad guy needs a support system, too. I've always believed that the worst people are just good people who have fallen off the rails, but I'm certain I'm getting back on the right track.

Chapter 10

Tony

I laugh right in Luca's face. "That's a spare!" One thing I've picked up over the past few months is the incredible sport of bowling. It's not as easy as I make it look, if we're being completely honest here.

Tonight, is my coworker's birthday, and Hannah said I could bring a plus one and I thought it'd be good for Luca to get out of the house for a bit. Plus, he doesn't even have to get up early tomorrow because he never works on the weekends, and I asked for tomorrow off because I know I'll be here until the ugly lights come on.

For whatever reason, Luca decided to tell me he's better at bowling than I am on the way over here, so I have made it my personal mission to kick everyone's ass tonight.

I was a little bit nervous about bringing Luca along tonight- and by a little, I mean I was draped over the toilet throwing up because I was extremely anxious. I love Luca and I also love my coworkers, but I also have two completely different personalities around them. With Luca, he's been seeing the serious side of me lately because all we seem to talk about is Insieme. The conversation ends up circling back to Giovanna, and then I either lose my cool or end up having a meltdown. When I'm with my coworkers, I'm the same old happy Tony that I always was before Insieme fell apart. I knew I had to let loose and have fun, but mixing the two seemed daunting to me, but I realized I was worrying over nothing because tonight has been nothing but drinking and laughter.

"Just admit that I'm better than you," I say, half slurring my words as I step up to the aisle and grab a ball.

Luca sighs with a laugh. "No!"

"Do it!"

Our arguing makes everyone else laugh, and suddenly, I'm brought back to the interviews where I wouldn't even try, yet the audience would laugh at everything I said. I was deemed as the comedian of Insieme, and that was enough to keep me satisfied.

I have come to realize that I was born to make people laugh, so that's why I say, "I should consider standup comedy."

I'm sure that's just the alcohol talking, but Hannah hypes me up. "Oh, my goodness, yes! I would pay good money to see you stand up and ridicule people in the audience any day of the week. You have to do it, T!" I receive a bunch of nods and smiles from all my other coworkers, and it makes my heart swell. But then I look at Luca, who is wearing a stone-cold expression.

I know exactly what he's thinking: people are not supposed to pay to see me do stand up, they're supposed to pay to see me sing.

Of course, my coworkers know exactly who I am. Sometimes customers will even ask for an autograph or just stare at me for a long time and as if I was in that band. When that happens, it does nothing but create an awkward conversation because I can't really say much on the Insieme topic to the public because Reen made us sign a non-disclosure contract.

"Y'all should just be happy that I give you a free comedy act every time we're together," I laugh, trying not to take Luca's reaction to heart. I know how much he misses Insieme, but isn't it over? The toxic management, the endless hours spent at the studio, the strict schedule, it's all behind us and we need to move on. Of course, I miss Insieme, but every day gets a little easier and I miss it a little less than I did the night before.

For the rest of the evening, I try to focus on bowling and win all of the games. I'm well over five shots deep at this point, and doing what I haven't done in a while, I'm officially giving the I Love You speech to Hannah.

"And I just want to say thank you again for inviting me and letting me bring a plus one," I say quickly. "I love you so much and cannot imagine working without you."

She laughs as she hugs me. "Thank you for coming tonight! I'll see you…" Both of our eyes go wide as we try to remember our schedule. "I'll see you sometime!" she finally says, giving up.

I laugh and then make my way to Luca. "Ready to head out?"

He nods his head. "I'm so tired, but tonight was so much fun."

"I know right, but we need some rest."

Luca, being the responsible one, already ordered an Uber, so all we have to do is walk out and find the car. Which should be an easy task, except I think it's a great idea to run away from Luca.

"Tony, the car is this way, you ding-dong," he hackles after me. I turn around, facing him as I job backwards.

"You got to catch me first."

Sometimes I forget that Luca was the one who played football and not me, so of course he catches up in no time and drags me to the car. He puts my seatbelt on for me and tells the driver our address. I don't really say anything the whole car ride, just laugh occasionally and rub it in some more that I beat him in bowling.

I have so much to say to him about moving on from Insieme, and I want to come clean, but the words get stuck in my throat. So, I laugh. I joke to avoid confrontation, simple as that.

But the truth is, I can tell Luca also has a lot to say by the way he puts his hands on our kitchen island as soon as we walk in. I want nothing more than to pass out on my comfy bed right now, but I know my best friend and I see that he needs this weight off of his chest.

"What's up?" I ask, sitting down on the bar stool across from him.

He hangs his head. "You know when you talked about being a standup comedian? All I could think about was Insieme. We were born to be on stage with the spotlight blinding us, we weren't meant for these nine to five jobs, T. I hate that we aren't on tour anymore."

How many times can one have the same conversation? "I don't want Insieme to get back together, if that's what you're getting out, Luca."

He squeezes his eyes shut, still unable to make eye contact with me. "I may or may not have called Samantha."

The hairs on the back of my neck stand up at the sound of her name. What made him decide that it would be good for us to get back with Reen? That's the equivalent of getting in bed with the devil, and I can't believe he would do that.

"You have a lot of explaining to do."

As he's explaining his phone call with Samantha, I can't tell if it's the alcohol or the fact that none of the windows are open, but I start to heat up. I undo one of my buttons on my shirt because I can't seem to breathe properly.

"Luca, we can't go back to Reen," I cut him off, not letting him continue on with the story.

"That's what Gia said."

Gia? He talked to Giovanna? Before me? "You already talked to her about this?" I shouldn't be surprised about this, that's how it always was- them, and *then* me.

"Yes, and she isn't willing to get sober on anyone's conditions."

"Okay, explain everything."

This time, I let him finish the full story, and I hate to admit it, but I'm with Giovanna on this one. If there's one thing we have in common, it's that we both hate Samantha.

"Luca, she isn't wrong." Is he even hearing how toxic it already sounds? Going back to a company unless she gets sober is ridiculous. Getting an alcoholic to get sober by forcing them to do so is definitely not a solution. I know that Gia hurt me, but she doesn't deserve that. No one deserves that. I can't believe the supposedly "love of her life" would even *consider* that.

"I know, but if that's what it takes to get Insieme back together, then we might just have to do it." Something in the way he shrugs his shoulders so casually makes my blood boil.

"Look." I shake my head. "Reen is not the end all be all. If you have intentions of getting

Insieme back together, you need to explore other options, because going back to Reen is insanity."

"But look at us! Reen could give us our tour back because everything is already set up with them; they know us," he pleads his case.

I slam my hands down. "Do you even care about Giovanna? Do you even care about *me*? Do you have absolutely any idea as to what Reen did to us?!"

It looks like fumes are steaming out of his ears. "Of course, I know, I lived through it!"

But you had it much better than I did, I want to say. Of course, not being able to get engaged is horrific and inhumane, but I was controlled from day one. I was silenced. It's too traumatic to talk about with Luca, but now I think that perhaps Giovanna would understand. Oh gosh, I must be really drunk if I just considered calling Giovanna.

"I'm beat, I'm going to bed. I know you miss Insieme, and maybe one day we'll get back together, but I'm telling you right now that Reen is not a good option."

I leave the kitchen and go to my bedroom without waiting for a response, and I sit on the edge of my bed with my phone in my trembling hand.

I really shouldn't, it's a bad idea. But people do stupid things when they're drunk, so I hit her number.

"Hello?" she says, picking up right away. I thought that she would be asleep, but I forgot about her sleep insomnia issues.

"Hey," I whisper, "sorry to bother you so late, but would you be able to meet tomorrow?"

I start to think that maybe I'm dreaming and talking to an imaginary person because all I hear is silence, but then I get: "I'd thought you'd never ask, Tony."

I can hear the smile in her voice, and despite how much she's hurt me, I know that I've missed her. She was my best friend after all, and best friends have bumps in the road just like everyone else. When that happens, the real question is this: who will be the first one to put their pride and ego aside and just pick up the damn phone?

In this case, I did, and that's how I fell asleep with a peaceful mind because I know that I will be able to have a conversation with Giovanna that I should have had ages ago.

Chapter 11

Giovanna

I can't say I'm surprised that Tony eventually called me, but I would say that I'm disappointed that I took so long to reach out. I was under the impression that when he said to never speak to him again, he meant that literally. I guess this just proves that Nancy was right about how people say irrational things when they're upset.

As I walk into the Starbucks that Tony picked, I see him already at a table with a drink in his hand. I start to panic- should I hug him, or should I just nod? But it's like he reads my mind and stands up, coming in for a hug. I forgot how good of a hugger Tony is.

"What are you drinking?" I ask, sitting down across from him.

"An Irish Cream Americano," he replies, puckering his lips after he takes a sip. "Would you like anything? Drinks are on me."

I smile at him. "Well, I'm still not much of a coffee drinker." I take a look up at the menu behind the barista, but I can't make out anything. All the grandees and the ventis always have and always will be like a second language to me, and I will never understand why they can't just say small, medium, or large.

"A white-hot chocolate it is," Tony decides for me with a nod of his head, getting up to the cashier before I have a chance and placing another order. He whips out a few coins and pays for me, so I thank him. It doesn't take long for the barista to make my drink and before I know it, I'm sitting down across from Tony with a piping hot drink in my hand.

He looks good. He's obviously been keeping up with his skincare routine because I don't see one bump or pimple in his perfect skin, and he seems bright and vibrant. As I look at the person with whom I share both good and bad memories with, I feel an immense amount of guilt.

"Tony, I just want to start off by saying sorry. I lost the deal, I messed up badly, but losing the deal wasn't the worst thing that I lost. I lost you, and I'm sorry for that. I'm sorry for everything." I know that no number of words will ever be enough for forgiveness, and I'm not looking for any, but I just need to at least let him know that I feel awful.

He takes a long sip from his drink and ponders over my words. "I know that you're sorry."

Knowing Tony, I was expecting him to say more, but nothing follows his statement. I will take what I can get, though, so I decide to carry on. "I'm not looking for us to move in together, but if we see each other on the street, a little nod would be enough for me," I say.

He nods his head. "My thoughts exactly."

I smile and clear my throat. Of course, I miss Luca because I wanted to marry him and I am still head over heels for him, but losing Tony was just as bad. It wasn't any better and I don't know if I'll ever be able to forgive myself for losing both of them.

"Why did you want to meet?" I ask the question that has been burning in my mind ever since I got his phone call.

He breaks eye contact with me and focuses on his coffee. "Luca told me he called Samantha again."

"He told me, too."

Tony looks me in my eyes. "Is it okay if I rant to you for a minute? I don't really know who else to go to right now." I watch as his shoulders tense up and my heart aches for him.

"Of course."

He inhales deeply like he used to do backstage before going on for our concerts. "You weren't the only one who was restricted under Reen's management."

This knocks the air right out of my lungs. "What are you saying, T?"

I already know it's going to be bad, but I'm not sure to what extent. I don't know if I'm prepared to hear it.

"For the first little bit, it was nice. It was- literally- a dream come true, but that was only before we started to do all the concerts. When we started to gain popularity and more eyes, we started to gain more and more eyes, so many eyes." He shudders. I often do the same thing in Nancy's office, and she says it's something called an anxiety shiver. Again, my heart aches for him.

"Samantha pulled me aside and she-" I lean in, straining to hear Tony because he's dropped his voice down as he whispers, "I don't know if I can say it."

I give him a small smile. "Take as long as you need." What else can I say?

He clears his throat and takes a few deep breaths. "She gave me the same reason she gave Luca as to why he couldn't put a ring on your finger. She told me that most of our fans were girls, and those girls were physically attracted to me."

I think I have an idea where he's going with this, but he needs to get it off his chest. I can tell he wants to say this himself, so I bite my tongue.

"She told me that since we had gained such a large fan base in a short amount of time, we couldn't risk it."

"Risk what?"

He focuses on his coffee again, unable to look at me. "She said we couldn't risk me getting into a public relationship."

"Oh."

"With a guy," he clarifies. "I don't know how she found out I was gay, and I mean, I'm not ashamed that I am. It's just that only you and Luca knew because you two were the only ones I fully trusted with that." He breathes again, getting choked up on his emotions.

I feel a wave of nausea come over me as I think about how much my actions affected him, and the fact that he saw me as someone who could keep his secrets and I basically spat on him. Of course, I don't want to take away from Tony's moment and tell him how sorry I am, so I remain silent and let him carry on.

"Imagine you're a twelve-year-old girl who is just starting puberty and you hear a song by Insieme on the radio for the first time. You look them up and realize that *that* Tony guy makes you feel some type of way. Sooner or later, you've got

Tony posters hung up on all corners of your room, you're the first person to like any of his posts, and you become completely obsessed with him. You even claim that you love him and that he's saved your life.

"But then one day, you look at your phone to see a new post from him, so you screech at the top of your lungs as you wait for a highly anticipated photo shoot of him. Except you see him with a guy. The caption reads 'spending time with my love' and you become confused. Surely, how could someone so good looking, so perfect for you, be *gay*? It's simply impossible, but it's in the picture so you know it has to be true. Your heart breaks into a million pieces and you've never felt such betrayal in your life, so you make a vow to never listen to Insieme again."

I hand him a napkin once I notice a tear has run down his cheek. "Tony, I'm so sorry." The way he explains that scenario makes me certain that those were Samantha's exact words when she told him to stop being who he is. "Why didn't you say anything to me?" I ask.

He shakes his head. "Everything was so new. We were about to go on tour and our first album had just been released, so we couldn't back out of the deal right then and there; I *knew* that. I was completely aware that you and Luca were having the time of your lives, and I was quite honestly jealous. I told myself that I needed to shake this off and carry on as if everything was normal. Remember that cute reporter I told you about and how I should have gotten his number?"

I think back to the press conference that was held to talk about our album. I could tell that the reporter was totally into Tony, and the feeling was obviously mutual. "Of course, I do."

"I knew I couldn't get his number because Samantha would've killed me if pictures came out of me talking to a guy." He shivers again. "I don't want to say that the whole time I was in Insieme, I was faking happiness. I was over the moon to sing with you guys, to tour, to party, and to just be with you and Luca, but I couldn't be *me*. It was confusing and I still have a hard time understanding it, and I'm not too sure if I'm going to recover from it. I mean, when is it my turn to get into a relationship?

"You and Luca were so cute together, and I know you guys have broken up and all, but I want what you guys had. I want to be able to walk out onto the street and hold a guy's hand without receiving dirty looks from strangers or losing thousands of fans. Sometimes, in the very late hours of the night, I think to myself *why can't I just live a normal life*? *How am I so different from everyone else?* I breathe, eat, and talk the same way as anyone else on this earth, yet Reen alienated me. I haven't been able to be in a serious relationship now because of them."

As I look at him, I realize how selfish I've been all these years to only talk about myself. "Hey, I get it, Luca and I couldn't get married, but your situation is worse. I'm so, so sorry."

"I really hate you for losing the deal because I think that you should have kept your emotions in check, especially since I've had to keep quiet about my sexuality for years and never drank away the contract. I'm upset that you were so ignorant and didn't care about how your actions affected me or Luca, but in some weird way, I'm thankful for it. Would I have much rather you had come to us and said 'I want out of the band'? Of course. I don't think the way you went about stabbing Luca and I in the back was right by any means, but I needed a break from Insieme. Or more, I needed a break from Reen because I absolutely loved you and I love Luca."

I notice how he says "loved" instead of "love", and I stupidly start to cry. "I don't know what else to say except that I'm really sorry, Tony."

"I just couldn't believe that one of the people I trusted the most would betray me like that and not even consider my feelings," he continues, and I don't blame him for ignoring my apology. "Look, you've done things that have damaged me quite a bit, but that doesn't mean I want to see you fail. I don't want you or me to go back to Reen, and I just wanted to see if we are on the same page."

I nod my head. "Of course, we are. I already told Luca that I won't even consider going back to Samantha because it was too toxic, but he didn't really like that."

Tony shrugs. "Samantha always favored Luca and I'm not trying to bash him, but it was painfully obvious. She would always call him first before us, she would laugh more at his jokes, and he started to get more and more lines in all of our songs."

He did have a great voice, but so did Tony and I. there was no reason for him to get a verse over me when it was my turn in the rotation to sing, but Samantha had the final say, I guess.

I snicker a little. "Isn't it weird? How many artists we listen to growing up and we idolized them; we wanted to be them. As soon as we became them, we were punched right between the eyes with reality, realizing that our favorite artists may have never had it easy at all."

"How many of them signed with Reen, though?" he questions. "I mean, I get where you're coming from, but I don't think all management companies are toxic. I think we just picked the wrong one."

I blame myself for picking up Samantha's call that day, it was my fault that I didn't properly research and just jumped into Reen head first. Although the boys were the one who wanted to drop out and not me, we were all fooling ourselves with that pipe dream. No sixteen-year-old is cut out for the harshness and competition of Hollywood.

"Tony, I know I keep saying it, but I am truly sorry that you had to go through that alone. I feel worse that I made it seem as though you couldn't come to me with this kind of thing. If you had told me this from the beginning, I would have beaten her up, you know that, right?"

He lets out a little laugh as he nods his head. "I know, Giovanna, but I also hope you can understand why I didn't tell you."

"Of course!" I clarify, and I don't know why my voice cracks.

I feel terrible that Tony was listening to me talk about my problems, and I didn't stop once to think about him. I tell Nancy all the time that Tony was my best friend, but I'm starting to see that it was a one-sided friendship, and I was and still am in the wrong.

"I'm sorry, by the way, that Luca gave you that proposal for the conditional deal." He clears his throat, preparing himself to talk about the elephant in the room.

I cast my eyes down. "I think I want to get sober, but I will not do it just because Samantha asked me to. I spent five years of my life following her rules, and it's time to stop. It's time to hold myself accountable and start my sobriety journey on my own terms."

"You don't know how glad I am to hear that, Gia," he comments.

I flash him a smile. "I've gotten so much wrong in my life, and I want to make things right. I don't know when or exactly how, but I promise you that I'll do everything I can to turn things around."

"You know I'll always be rooting for you," he whispers with a beaming smile on his face.

"Let me just tell you my thought process right now, so everything is laid out for you. I think Insieme may get back together someday, but I definitely know we will not sign with Reen. At least, I won't be in Insieme if Samantha is involved."

He extends his hand for me to shake. "Well, shake on it then, so you can stick to your word because I truly hope with everything in me that you're correct."

I laugh as I shake his hand; I've missed him and can't believe I lost him.

I just need to get back in line first. For so many years I've been flying by the seat of my pants, but now I know exactly what I have to do to make these coffee dates with Tony a daily occurrence.

Step number one: get sober.

Part Two

Chapter 12

Giovanna

I accept the tissue that Nancy passes me. "I'm just tired of failing." Again, with the poor me act, I know, but I'm going to say exactly how I feel because Nancy will never judge me.

She gives me the time to let out all of my sobs. "What happened?"

One thing I've noticed about Nancy and her questions is that she will ask because she already knows the answer. I think she does that to get me to say exactly how I feel and admit my emotions, plus she doesn't want to assume my feelings.

"I relapsed again," I hush through my tears.

Ever since my meeting with Tony, we've shared the occasional texts. Is it bad that I talk to Tony more than I talk to Luca? Of course, I miss my ex-boyfriend, but I don't know. I thought I wanted to marry him, but did I ever have the chance to experience a relationship with anyone else? He's all I've ever known since I was sixteen, so I thought he would be there for me at my lowest, not cut all ties and leave me as if I never meant anything to him.

The media put a lot of pressure on Luca and I to stay together, and I think that's part of the reason we worked through our problems, or tried to work through them, at least. We didn't want to deal with the drama of a public breakup, but that plan backfired when I threw our contract away. We were right though, because the amount of hate I've received ever since Insieme broke up is concerning.

"I really didn't mean to relapse," I say. "I want to get sober, but it's just... I don't know how to explain it."

She squints her eyes. "What part about it do you find challenging?"

I shrug. "I've been drinking since I was sixteen, so it's become part of my daily routine. I never consciously made the decision to walk to the fridge and grab myself a drink; it was just natural. Now that I'm trying to stop, I've started to have more panic attacks. I find myself walking to my bottles and then I just freeze on the spot. I want to turn around, and for two days, I was able to walk away."

"Two days?" she asks, no hint of judgment in her voice at all.

"I couldn't even make it for three days," I admit. "It's embarrassing, actually."

"Why are you embarrassed?" she asks. "Expecting to get sober right away is unrealistic."

"I haven't been able to stay sober for more than seventy-two hours!" I wail, frustrated with no one but myself.

"I know you're frustrated, but this isn't a race. This is about you getting better, and you will, but it's going to be slow and steady."

I shake my head. "It's all I can think about, really. I feel terrible when I'm not drinking, but I feel terrible when I do drink, so I have no idea what to do. I feel like a hamster on a wheel."

Lost. I feel lost.

Nancy picks up her cup of coffee. "Have you considered getting a job?"

I shake my head. "I couldn't do that."

"Why not?"

I shoot her a look. "Do you know what kind of attention that will draw to me? People can't just walk into a random store on a Monday and see that the once famous pop star is now working there. They'll say that I'm an even bigger failure than they already do."

"You told me that Tony and Luca got jobs, though," she states blatantly. "What's the harm if you do?"

I know she has a point, but I'm still hesitant. "Look, fans are growing more and more impatient by the second. They're spamming my social media, asking when a reunion is going to happen or if Insieme is done for good. Reen put out a public statement for us that we have taken a break, but the three of us can't address anyone about it. If they see me at a job, they won't leave me alone until they get their answer, and I won't know what answer to give them."

She looks at me and then takes the longest blink known to mankind. "Do you think that maybe you're in your own head a little bit? The boys work jobs, and between the two of them, Tony is exposed to hundreds of strangers. We don't see him getting swarmed when he's bussing a table, do we?"

I shrug. "We never know." I know she's right, but a job- the real world- seems scary to be perfectly honest, because it just solidifies that Insieme is over for good.

"Luca came to you and said there would be a deal back on the table, and you didn't even hear him out, which I'm proud of you for. Going back to Reen would be the worst possible thing you could do right now, especially being forced into sobriety. However, that means that the Insieme door has closed and it's time to move on. I think a big part of the reason as to why you can't seem to get sober is because you don't have somewhat of a distraction. From what you describe, you get up, occasionally come to me, and then stay in your motel room for the rest of the day."

"I agree that it'll be good, but-"

"You don't want Insieme back, but yet you're still living as though you're still in it."

I clear my throat. Nancy doesn't get brutally honest often, but when she does, it makes my throat tight. "I want Insieme back together, I just don't want to go back to Reen," I clarify. "Yes, I am still living like Insieme is still a thing because it was all I ever had. I don't think you understand how much that group meant to me, and I threw it all away because I couldn't keep my hands off the damn bottle, and now look at me! I'm sitting here ranting to some stranger that I barely know, getting judged by an outsider looking in, and the worst part is that I actually care about what you have to say," I cry out.

She stares at me once I pause and I'm certain she's going to say something, but she remains silent and allows me to do all the talking.

"I don't need you or anyone else pointing out how much of a failure I am, because I already know that I am. That stupid group was the only thing that kept me grounded and I lost it. I lost my boyfriend, I lost my best friend, and I lost my career. The only way to get them back is to get sober, but it's just so hard."

"It *is* possible, Giovanna. It's just going to take some time and a little bit of patience, and I also think getting a job will tremendously help you."

"I know, but I'm just frustrated," I say.

"Perhaps you need to fix your mindset."

I feel rage building up more and more inside of me, but I try to keep my cool. Does she honestly think that I've never thought of that? "How so?"

"You don't have to tell me if you don't want to, but why do you *really* want to get sober?"

I let out a frustrated sigh, as if I haven't just spent the past thirty minutes explaining my answer to that question. "I told you it's because I need the boys back."

"Interesting."

She offers nothing more or less, so I continue to talk. "I've told you that plenty of times."

"And if all of those times you've yet to see the root of the issue," she fires back matter-of-factly.

I huff and cross my arms. "Enlighten me."

"When Luca approached you, you told him that you wanted to get sober on your own terms and conditions. So doesn't that mean that you need to get sober for you and nobody else?"

I stare at her. My first thought is that she should have just told me that from the beginning, and then I take a step back and start to breathe. I count five seconds in and five seconds out, just like I've been taught.

Why am I getting sober? To get Insieme back.

And what happens when Insieme gets back together? I'll relapse in a matter of seconds because I would have pleased the boys enough that I would be less strict with my rules. I can envision it now- the terrible relapse and a dramatic ending to Insieme yet again.

So why else do I want to get sober? Why do I *really* want to get sober?

"I don't like who I am when I drink; I can't limit myself. At the start, I'm fun, but then I start to get angrier and angrier as the night goes on. I get mad and say things that I shouldn't, and I end up feeling terrible about it. Just terrible. Everyone can see it, even my family, so I want to get sober for myself. I don't want to feel like every day is hard."

She nods her head and a slight smile spreads across her face. "Now we're getting somewhere."

The fact that Nancy can see some progress being made, even though I necessarily can't, makes me gain a little more confidence. It may not happen now, but as long as I put one foot in front of the other, I might be able to slowly turn my life around.

Chapter 13

Luca

It feels wrong being here. Tony told me that I owed it to myself to be here tonight, and I think this is one of those times where I should have never listened to him.

Sitting here across from Christina feels like I'm committing a crime. The only thing I'm thinking about is how I can't wait to go home and take a shower to get this filthy feeling off of me.

"I don't really know what I want to do with my life, but I'm just taking it one day at a time right now," she says. I didn't even ask her. In fact, I think I've said maybe a total of three words tonight.

Here's how I ended up here: I was waiting in line with Tony at the movie theater to get popcorn because Tony dragged me out of the house. He told me that he's tired of spending his nights alone with me, so I listened to him and agreed to go to the movies. All of a sudden, I felt a tap on my shoulder that made me jump. When I turned around, there was this brunette girl smiling at me and I was brought back to getting swarmed by thousands of fans in Los Angeles. To some extent, she is just a fan, but I was not expecting her to suggest that we should go out sometime. When I gave Tony a look that was a clear sign for help, he did nothing but smile and encourage me.

Which is how I ended up here a day later, sitting across from a girl whose last name I don't even know. And the worst part? She wanted to *share* dinner. Giovanna would have never asked me to share my shrimp tacos with her, probably because she was full from her burger, but I loved that about her. After dating her for over four years, it feels unnatural to sit across from someone other than her.

"What do you think?" she asks, and the only reason I hear her is because for the first time tonight, she has stopped talking. Then I realize that it's my turn to say something, but I have no idea what she's talking about because I completely tuned her out.

I clear my throat. "Sorry, what was that? The music is very loud in here," I say, trying to cover up the fact that I have no interest in this one-sided conversation.

She giggles as if me not paying attention to her is somehow funny. "I asked your opinion on what I should do with my family wanting me to go back to school." I don't even know her and she thinks that talking about the fact that she's a college dropout is a good "first date" conversation. Bizarre.

I shrug my shoulders. "I don't know."

She smiles as she looks at me. "My thoughts exactly."

Is this girl for real? Does she not know how to read the room and notice how uninterested I am right now?

I check my watch and am disappointed to see that it's only 6:30. The only thing I want to do is dash out of here- maybe even leave her with the bill- and then call Giovanna.

"I'm having such a fun time!" she exclaims, to which I respond with a nod of my head and a fake smile.

The truth is, I haven't given a genuine smile since the day Giovanna walked out the door.

I was forced to let her go, and Tony suggested that maybe the only way for me to be happy again is to move on. But how can I move on from her? The only person who ever understood me on a deeper, intimate level? She was the only person who knew what I needed before the words even left my mouth.

"How is everything tasting over here?" The waiter asks, maybe even being my saving grace.

"Fine."

"Can I grab anything else?"

"No." I don't know why Christina is being so rude, and I wish the waiter would have stayed at our table longer so I could apologize for her snarky behavior.

"Is everything okay, Luca?" Christina asks, forcing me to snap out of my thoughts again. "You're very quiet."

I look at her, wondering if there's a way to let her down easily. If I tell her the truth about how I've had a terrible time here, she'll run her mouth to the press for sure. I don't want to lead her on though, because if I tell her that I've had a wonderful time, she's bound to ask me for another date, and that's just out of the question.

I shake my head. "I'm just tired." Which directly translates to *get me out of her as fast as possible*.

She lets out a small gasp, as if she couldn't tell already. "Should we get going then?"

I thought you'd never ask. "Yeah."

She flags down the waiter, and that's my final straw. She could have waited patiently like I did and smiled at the waiter, after all, they have to deal with so much crap for eight hours. After the horror stories that Tony's told me about his hospitality industry experiences, I view waiters in a different light. I'm mad at Christina that she can't see how privileged she is and that she basically called him over like a dog.

"Why did you do that?" I ask, letting my emotions get the best of me. Sure, I may just be looking for something to fight about with her, but the fact of the matter is that I hate everything about her.

"Do what?" she laughs, signaling the waiter over again because he didn't see her the first time.

"Would you cut it out, please? Our server isn't a dog, he's a human being with emotions that deserves to be treated with respect."

"Why are you getting so upset right now?" Annoyance has crept into her voice, feeding my anger even more.

"Because he served you hand and foot all night and you think you can just call him over with a snap of your fingers."

She cocks her head to the side. "I asked you if you wanted to go and so I thought I would ask for the bill."

I let out a sigh. "I've wanted to go the whole night, but you don't see me practically cat-calling him, do you?"

I shouldn't have said that. I should have kept my temper in check and shut my mouth like I was trained to do by Reen. Instead, I exploded like I always do, and now I feel every set of eyes in this restaurant land on our table as Christina gathers her things as dramatically as possible.

"I should have known you were an asshole!" She pushes her chair back and it screeches loudly against the hardwood floor.

As if. She's treating me like we've been dating for like ten years, but I know I'm not a bad guy. I've just had enough of everything right now in my life. Should I be taking everything out on Christina? Maybe not, but she certainly has not helped my emotions at all, and it's not my fault she can't take a hint.

"Look, I'm sorry, I thought it would be a good idea to come here tonight, but I shouldn't have."

"Do you even like me?" The way she says it with such pain makes me confused, did she think this was something serious?

I wouldn't say she's terrible by any means, but she's not Giovanna. And I only have eyes for Giovanna Rossi.

"It's complicated," I reply.

That's enough for her to throw her napkin at me and storm out of the restaurant. Finally, the waiter comes over wearing a surprised look on face. "Sir, I just wanted to say that I'm so sorry for how poorly she treated you. I think you did a wonderful job, and I apologize for making a huge scene. May I please get the bill?"

He nods his head. "I appreciate that, and you were wonderful to deal with. Between you and me, I didn't think she was worth your time anyways."

I want to talk to him more and ask him what he means, but he leaves to get the bill. Then I remember that just because I may not be touring anymore, people still know who I am. Everyone has this preconceived notion of me- whether that's Christina or a waiter.

When he comes back, I make sure to tip him well and then I head out the door. I should call a taxi or Tony to get a ride home, but I need to take a walk to clear my head. I don't necessarily know where I'm headed, but I just start walking, moving onwards and upwards.

I start to think about Giovanna, of course. She was and *still* is the love of my life. I told her I can't believe I fell in love with an alcoholic, but what kind of man did that make me? Especially if I claimed to have loved her so much, I should have helped her, should have held her tighter and reassured her. I could have eased her into therapy, rather than just throwing her to the sharks. I could have saved her.

I wish things were different.

I wish that I could walk right into a home, maybe with four or so bedrooms, and find her on the couch. She would probably be watching *A*

Bronx Tale and I would kiss her. I would embrace her and kiss her as if tomorrow will never come.

Sitting across from Christina, I realize just how much I miss her. Her scent, her lips, her body, everything. The way we were a perfect fit, the way we knew each other's movements and what each of us liked or didn't.

I can't just pick up the phone and call her now, what good would that do? That would only confuse both of us even more, but...

I want her.

It's always been her, but things are different now. We're not who we used to be, and it makes me sick to my stomach.

Have you ever felt like you're at a crossroad where you're deciding to go either left or right? You don't know what outcome will come out of both of them, but that's the difference between you and I. In fact, I know exactly what I'll find at the end of the left and right road.

Giovanna and I will find our way back to each other. I'm just unsure if I should go left- the path where I ask for her back. Where I forgive her instantly and hold her tight, letting her know that I forgive her for that pain she caused me. I would do that because I know that my life is much better with her than without her. I want to let her know that I could have and *should* have treated her much better than I did- all the petty fights were not truly worth it, looking back now.

I could get her back right now.

Or I could turn right. I could wait it out, twiddle my thumbs while she does her own self-discovery journey. I can wait and let her eventually apologize, let her make amends, and let her come back to me on her own terms.

Except I'm not patient, we all know about my anger issues. I'll yell at someone if they call a waiter over with a snap of their fingers, so patience is not a virtue that I have.

I should reach out, at least, because she needs to know that she has a support system behind her. She has me, and I'm sure she has Tony, but I'm not entirely certain if she knows that we're still in her corner. And that's our fault.

Here's where we're at right now: we're in the boxing ring. It's me and Tony in Gia's coaching corner, urging Gia on to go one more round. But you see, Gia isn't fighting Samantha, or Reen, or even an asshole like John Feton. She's fighting herself. She's fighting the darker parts of her that need to be fixed. Her inner demons.

So, as I pick up my phone, knowing that Giovanna is in desperate need for some water in this ten rough fight, I already know that I'm turning left.

Chapter 14

Giovanna

I'm walking over to the fridge, about to crack open a beer, when my phone rings. I pause mid stride, unsure if I should just let it ring and continue or if I should pick it up. I shut my eyes, willing every bone in my body to turn around and pick up the phone. I just need a drink, that's all, but I decide it can wait and head towards my buzzing phone on the counter.

I can't help the smile that breaks onto my face when I see Luca's name. I feel like an awkward teenager all over again, giddy with emotions. I remember purposely dressing up for him, wondering if he would notice that my earrings are just a little bit bigger, my clothes are just a little bit tighter, or that I even put on perfume for him. As Awkward and weird as our relationship was at the beginning, I believe that it was still true love, even if it was just puppy love.

"Hello," I say, sounding happier than usual.

"Giovanna." He sounds almost relieved to say my name, like his lips have been sealed for ages and he can finally speak again.

"Is everything alright?" I ask, going into panic mode. I snap out of my fantasy, perfect world for a moment, remembering that Luca and I are separated and have not so much as held hands in months. Why else would he be calling me if there wasn't an emergency?

There's a long pause and I start to wonder if our phone connection has dropped, but then I hear him sigh. "I went on a date."

I take a seat on the couch. I don't know what I was expecting- maybe a family emergency, maybe an apology, or maybe even another pitch to get Insieme back together. But this. No, I wasn't expecting this at all. His sentence cuts me like a knife, and I start to wonder if maybe Luca is an evil man, or even a man at all. What kind of boy calls their ex-kind-of-fiancé to tell them they went on a date with another woman? Not someone with respect, I'll tell you that much.

I clear my throat, trying to come up with words, but none come out. "Oh," I say, unable to formulate a proper sentence.

He lets out a small laugh that infuriates me because I'm not really sure what's so funny in this situation. "I hated it. I hated it so much, Giovanna. She actually stormed out on me at the end."

Just like that, my heart starts to rejuvenate, but I don't want to get my hopes up just yet. "Okay," I say, trying not to show all of my cards. If I could do summersaults, I would have done twenty in a row by now, but gymnastics was never my strong suite.

"Yeah," he laughs, "it was terrible. I don't know what to say to you, but I needed to call you and let you know that I thought about you every second I was sitting across from Christina."

Christina, I think, *he went out with a girl named Christina?* Don't get me wrong, I absolutely adore Christina Aguilera and I think she's an icon, but I don't like that name right now for understandable reasons. I want to ask him so many questions like how he even ended up there, and why we would even say yes in the first place, or perhaps he asked her out. But I can't seem to find my voice, and I don't want to hurt my own feelings.

"Do you mind sending me your motel address?"

I take a look around at the piles of clothes on the floor and the numerous empty bags on my counter that should have gone in the garbage weeks ago. "It's a mess in here, Luca, I don't think you should-"

"Please," he practically begs. "Please, I just need to see you. I don't care what kind of mess you have there, all that matters is that I'm with you."

I sigh reluctantly. "I'll send you my address."

"I'll be there in two minutes," he replies before hanging up the phone. I don't know exactly what just happened, but all I know is that I have one messy room to clean up.

When I hear the knock on the door, I feel a sudden wave of self-consciousness. I don't know why I felt the need to put on a silk button up shirt and jeans that hug me in all the right places, but there's no turning back now. I feel overdressed and quite honestly a little silly that I thought I needed to dress up for Luca.

As I open the door, I'm hit with a sense of relief that he's in a button up as well. "Come on in," I say, urging him inside. "Can I get you anything to drink?"

He studies me and I burn under his gaze; I've missed his eyes. "What do you have?"

"Pretty much anything you want," I say truthfully with a shrug.

He opens his mouth, ready to tell me, but then he shuts it again and scrunches his eyebrows together. "I'll just have water," he says with a soft smile.

I nod and make my way to the fridge and pull out a bottle of water for him. For months, I've told Nancy how much Luca hates me, but now, I can feel the tension between us. It's the good kind of tension, the kind where you can tell how badly you long to be in each other's arms.

"A water for you, too?" he asks, raising his eyebrow up. I can't tell if he's skeptical or impressed.

I nod my head. "Trying to stay clean for a while."

A small, very faint smile appears on his lips. "That's amazing, Gia. I'm proud of you."

There it is. The only four words anyone wants to hear from someone they love. *I'm proud of you*. I have goosebumps running up and down my body because it excites me that I've finally gotten one thing right between us in months.

"Sorry I showed up here with such short notice."

"It's no bother," I say at the same time he says, "I just needed to see you."

I laugh, amused by how the more things change, the more they stay the same. I stare at my fridge as silence comes over us, wishing with every bone in my body that I could have just one sip of alcohol. I would be less awkward, it'll make me happier, and it will comfort me in this tense situation. Although I'm glad to have him here, I'm not sure exactly how to handle it, and I know a drink will help. I don't think I've been able to manage a problem or situation sober since I was 16.

"Luca," I whisper, "what are we doing here?"

"I'm not sure, but I don't want to leave," he says, matching my whisper tone.

"I don't want you to go either," I admit over the pound of my heart. "Is it a good idea for you to be here, though?"

"We put ourselves in quite the pickle here, didn't we?" he says with a smirk. I know it was meant to come across as flirty, or even suggestive, but it just makes my heart sink.

"No, I messed everything up," I clarify. "I'm so sorry, Luca. For everything."

He puts a single finger to my lips, stopping me mid apology and sending shivers down my spine. "Sometimes, *Amore*, actions say a million times more than any word can."

He leans into me, hesitant but sure at the same time. I lean into him, wondering why I'm not putting an end to this. He kisses me softly. I've felt his lips on mine for five years, and tasting them after months apart feels better than waking up on Christmas Day to find gifts wrapped under the tree. He leans farther into me, laying me down on my back as he runs his fingers through my hair.

I can feel the wall I've built up come crumbling down. I'm done denying that I miss him and acting like I know it's better to stay away from him right now. The truth is, I want him back.

"We shouldn't be doing this, Gia," he whispers against my lips. I laugh at him, knowing full well that neither of us are going to stop. "I know, but I often find that bad things are actually what makes me feel so good."

As I get swept up into my perfect utopia world with Luca next to me, all of my worries fade away. My body seems to come alive, creating a greater buzz than any drink has ever given me.

I don't think any relationship is perfect, and I don't think by any means that Luca and I are picture-perfect. All I know is that when we are good, we are *really* good. We never were and we never will be perfect, but now, wrapped up in his arms, I feel an overwhelming amount of joy. It's pilling higher and higher on my chest, weighing me down like an anchor on a boat.

Chapter 15

Giovanna

I wake up to Luca's lips pressed against my forehead. "Good morning, Gia," he whispers with a scratchy throat.

I close my eyes, reality hitting me faster than a train. I can't bring myself to respond to him because I'm too confused.

"Are you alright?" he asks softly, brushing a tear from my eye. I hate that I'm crying and ruining such a beautiful moment between us.

"Yeah, it's stupid," I say, shaking my head.

He cups my hand in my face. "I don't think anything you say is stupid."

I cock my head to the side and click my tongue to the roof of my mouth. "You and I both know that's not true." Just like that, I'm not wrapped up in hotel room sheets, cuddling with Luca. I'm right back in Los Angeles, stumbling home from a bar and finding out that I lost the deal. I am sitting on my driveway sobbing like a baby and wishing with everything in me that I could be anyone else.

He snickers, dropping his hand from my face. "You're right; you like mint chocolate chip ice cream."

It breaks my heart to ask him the question that kept me up all night as I look at his beaming smile. "Luca, what are we now?" I whisper.

He shuts his eyes. "I don't know."

"It's not that I don't miss you, but I just-"

"Aren't ready for a relationship," he finishes for me.

I give him a sad smile. "I need to get better before I ruin your life again."

"I don't need you to be perfect," he says.

I look directly into his eyes. "I wish that I could be normal. I don't think you can ever understand how desperately I want to be good enough for you, but I can't be. Luca, I want to be at a mental and physical point in my life where I can be in a healthy relationship where I'm not a burden." Another tear streams down my cheek, hitting my lips with a salty splash.

His eyes dart back and forth as he stares back at me. "I had to come back for you, Gia."

I shut my eyes and turn my head slowly to the side, unable to look at his burning eyes. "I'm glad you did, but-"

"What kind of man would that make me, Giovanna?" he asks. "I love you. I love you with every damn part of me. When I wake up and when I fall asleep, I think of you every second of the day. I don't want the Christinas or the Brittanys in the world, I only want *you*. What kind of man would that make me if I left you all alone again?"

"I know you don't want to, but you have to let me do this on my own. You have to let me get better and figure out my life without babysitting me," I respond.

He shakes his head. "I lost you once, I will not lose you again."

"I'm just asking for a little bit of time," I hush sympathetically. "I know how much I hurt you, and it was never my intention to mess everything up, so I need to fix myself before I ruin your life again."

"I would still like to spend time with you, though," he says, lacing his fingers with mine.

"Me, too. I have a therapy session in a little bit, but I'll text you when I'm free," I assure him.

He leans in and kisses me. "Would you like a ride to your appointment?"

"That's alright, I don't want to bother you."

He smiles. "I never work on Saturdays; let me give you a ride."

It's not that I don't want a ride from him, it's just that getting into a car with someone I know after a therapy session is extremely awkward. Plus, I need time to process everything right now.

"It's honestly okay. I enjoy listening to music before and after my sessions- it gives me time to think about what Nancy has to say and what's going on in my life."

I know I used to be a singer and a great songwriter, but I'm not Bryan Adams or Bruce

Springsteen. The artists I grew up listening to have a way of writing songs that hit home and describe exactly what I'm feeling. No matter how bad my life is, if I plug in my earbuds and put them in at max volume, the pain is instantly gone.

I talk about the boys and my family saving my life, and even Nancy, but music has truly saved my life and remained constant. Whether it's writing a song, listening to music, or buying CDs, music always helps. Music has been and always will be a part of my life; it's like pure serotonin pumped straight into my veins.

I just wish music didn't also ruin my life.

"I understand that, no worries. Please text me when you're done, okay?" he asks.

"Of course," I reply with a smile.

He gets up and gathers his car keys and wallet and heads to the door. He pauses as his hand reaches the door knob and turns back around. "I love you, Gia, and I'm sorry I was never able to communicate that."

Before I'm able to respond, he walks out, leaving me sitting on my bed with my jaw on the floor.

Chapter 16

Giovanna

"You're in a great mood this morning," Nancy comments, handing me a mug of piping hot tea. I accept the mug, if only to hide my gushing. "How have things been?"

"Good!" I say a little too quickly. She turns her head to the side skeptically, waiting for me to elaborate. Unconsciously, I mirror her actions and tilt my head. "Things have been good." She doesn't say anything, she just squints her eyes at me and waits for me to explain myself. "Luca came over last night."

She nods her head. "Tell me about that."

I shrug my shoulders, trying to hide my red cheeks. "He went on a date yesterday, and I guess he realized how much he missed me. He called me afterwards and asked to see me, so one thing led to another."

"Did he spend the night?"

"Yes."

She writes something down in her notebook. "And do you think you're ready to get back together with him?"

I shoot my eyes to the ground. "See, that's where I'm unsure. I know that I feel good with him, but I don't think I'm ready for a relationship again, if that makes any sense?"

I feel like a crazy woman whenever I say that because if I truly love him, one would think that I would just get over myself and get back together with him. In fact, I know that I'm absolutely insane for shutting the door to my heart that Luca is so desperately knocking on, but I just can't open it. At least, not yet.

"I think that makes sense," she says. That's honestly one of the things I like the most about my sessions with Nancy- the way she makes me feel seen, heard, and understood.

"I have a lot of healing to do, and I have to admit, Nancy, that I was about to relapse again last night. I was literally about to crack open a can right before Luca called me, so I didn't, but I was about to."

She scribbles that down in her notebook again. "Does Luca know that you aren't quite ready to get back together?"

I nod my head. "We talked about it, though it wasn't an easy conversation. I just know he was disappointed and that he wants to be by my side while I go through this journey. He doesn't like that I'm starting to get sober by myself."

I swear I see a smile come across her face, as if she knows something I don't. "And what do you think of that? Do you think you would like someone by your side?"

The answer should be easy, shouldn't it? It should be a resounding YES! On a sign with flashing red lights. Does anyone *really* want to walk a new path of life on their own? I don't think so. Yet I can't bring myself to say yes. I just can't.

"I love him," I say, trying to explain myself as best as I can. "I really do love him, but…"

"But?"

I shake my head, frustrated that I can't find the words to articulate my feelings. "I've gone through a lot in my life. Whether I brought on those problems myself or if someone else caused them, all I know is that I have issues. But you know what I've realized? I can't be dependent on people because they will always- *always*- let me down.

"May that be my family, my friends, Luca, or anyone else, they will always let me down. It's inevitable that they'll disappoint me in the end. I will set my expectations of them way too high and they will inevitably fall short and I will be heartbroken again. I'm tired of having that happen. I know I say I've been through a lot, but I've yet to handle a problem by myself. I'm always relying on people to fix my life for me, and I want that to stop."

"It's okay, Giovanna, you're doing great," she encourages me when I pause to take a breather and recollect myself, dabbing my eyes with a tissue.

I swallow back some more tears as I carry on. "Hollywood painted me as this strong woman who didn't take shit from anyone, but I think I'm the exact opposite of that, actually. I truly believe that. I don't stand up for myself, and when I do, I can never keep my emotions in check. Other people feel responsible for me, so I need to change. I need to truly change before I get back together with Luca. I need to get sober, continue my sessions with you, and get myself back on my feet."

"And how does that relate to not getting back into a relationship?" she asks, even though I'm pretty sure she already knows the answer.

"I cannot and will not put Luca in the babysitter position again. This is an uphill climb- getting sober and then getting my career back- but I'm willing to do it. So my answer to your question is that I want to walk this battle against my own demons alone this time."

When I look back up at her, I'm surprised to see a satisfied look on her face. "Giovanna, I'm so proud of you. You're making excellent progress, but I think we can still work on self-kindness a little bit. I think you're strong, even though you don't see it yourself."

I smile at her. "Every time I see you, my life gets a little bit better and I feel a little bit stronger."

"That's my job, and I'm glad you think I'm doing a good one. So, tell me more about your night, tell me everything that's on your mind. I know you said you want to fight this battle alone, but just know that I'll be with you every step of the way."

"Wouldn't want it to be any other way," I beam, fully prepared to give her every small detail about what's happening in my life right now. It feels like a weight has been lifted off my chest as I continue to climb up this mountain I must overcome.

Chapter 17

Tony

"Oh. My. Wow." To say I'm at a loss of words would be a tremendous understatement. Luca and Giovanna, who would have thought? Everyone, I guess, and maybe even me, but I didn't think it would be this soon. I certainly wasn't expecting to be told he spent the night with Giovanna when I asked him how his date with Christina went.

"Tony, what do I do? Will we ever be able to go back to how it was?" he asks, bringing his hands to his face and shaking his head.

I can't help but laugh at him. "Someone is going to get a song written about him," I chide.

He slaps my arm. "Okay, that's enough from you."

"Hey! I'm not the one who went to see her last night." I put my arms up in defense.

He laughs as if he can't believe it himself as well. "I told her I wanted to get back together, and she just straight up rejected me, T!" he exclaims.

I shake my head. "I wouldn't say she flat out rejected you. This can still be shaved." Ish.

"No. No, this is bad." He shakes his head fast. "I can't believe this is happening."

I shrug my shoulders. "What's done is done, not much we can do about it now." I probably shouldn't ask this, but I do it anyway because that's just how I am. So, what does this mean for Insieme?"

He sucks on his teeth. "I don't know, man, it's just all so confusing. I don't know if she'll ever consider going back to Reen, you know?"

"Rightfully so," I say, defending Giovanna and myself. "I don't even want to sign with Reen again."

He nods his head. "I know, but like, what other option do we have? What other label would want to sign us with the kind of reputation we have?"

"I know you don't mean any harm, Luca, but you can't just ask us to go back to Reen. I've had a few conversations with her, and I told her my reason as to why I don't want to sign with them again."

"And why is that?" he asks.

I take a few deep breaths because I realize I can't keep avoiding this conversation. "They wouldn't let me publicly date a man because they told me it was bad for our reputation."

At this, Luca sits down on the couch, as if the words physically hurt him. "Why didn't you tell me, T?"

I shake my head. "It was complicated."

"What did they say exactly?"

I tell him everything from the beginning, and it pains me to see how hurt he is that I didn't tell him. He assures me that he will always be there for me and the whole nine yards, but then he turns the conversation back to Giovanna.

"Do you think she can change?" I know it shouldn't, but it upsets me that he just apologized for what happened to me and carried on about what was bothering him. It seems insensitive and selfish of him.

"I don't know."

"I'm just not really sure what to do with her right now. We saw each other last night, and now I'm not sure exactly what we are, and I need to get back to singing because if I spend one more damn day on the jobsite with my dad, I think that I'll gauge my eyes out, and I don't know what to do with my life right now if I don't have a record deal, and-"

"Calm down."

"What if I never get my old life back? Tell me what I'm supposed to do if-"

"Calm down." I grind my teeth, trying not to explode on him and ask him why he's not comforting me.

"I just feel so... tired. I'm tired of not knowing what tomorrow is going to be like, and-"

"CALM DOWN," I yell at him, shaking him by the shoulders. Obviously, I knew that Luca wanted Insieme back together- the whole world wants us back together- but I didn't know he had such strong feelings. And severe signs of depression.

"I'm sorry, I didn't mean to ramble on like that. I'm so sorry, Tony." I can hear him choking on his tears as he speaks, trying to hold them in.

"We don't always have to talk about some woman, because at the end of the day, God bless her soul, but Giovanna is just a woman," I say, frustrated that he disregarded my feelings.

He nods his head back and forth as he contemplates. "I mean, she is and she isn't. Mauve I'm naive in thinking that I'm going to marry her because she was my first girlfriend, but-"

"She wasn't the first girl you dated," I cut him off.

He rolls his eyes. "The first *serious* girlfriend I had," he clarifies. "It's so hard to explain, but I just wish we could get married right now."

"We can't keep having the same conversation, Luca. I don't think she ever stopped loving you. Sure, she maybe started to love alcohol more than she loved anything, but her love for you never went away and everyone sees that. I know that we don't have management holding us back anymore, but you can't marry her now. Not only do you owe it to her to figure her life out, you owe it to yourself to make sure that if you get married, you'll actually become a husband and not a caretaker."

"A little harsh, T," he whispers with a little wince.

Harsh? What's harsh is that I'm constantly offering him advice and lending an ear to him, only for him to brush off my rants as if they aren't that serious.

"That doesn't make it any less true, Luca. We have to stop having this conversation about how much you miss her. The fact of the matter is that it's too fragile of a situation right now to jump back into a relationship."

"I guess so," he says, sounding disappointed with what I had to say.

"If you want Insieme back together, then we have to give Gia space to sort her stuff out and start coming up with songs of our own."

"You know how I feel about song-writing," he says, fear taking over his face in a matter of seconds.

I don't know why he hates writing songs so much. I don't know whether it's because he thinks Giovanna writes better ones, or maybe he thinks everything he writes is stupid, but I need to see him at least try. To be completely honest, it aggravates me that he so desperately wants Insieme to get back together, yet he's unwilling to adapt and try something new to get to that point.

Now, do I think that out of the three of us Giovanna was the best writer? Of course. There's no denying that she made a hit when she was sixteen-years-old, and Luca and I relied heavily on her to create song after song. While Luca's talent is mostly in the instrumental side of our work, I think it's important for him to experiment and try something new.

"If you want Insieme back together, we can't just go to Giovanna and ask her to write all our songs for us. If I was her, I wouldn't want anything to do with us if we tell her that we miss singing, yet don't have any song ideas written down. It may be new, but whether you like it or not, we're going to sit down together and write some lyrics. We may write the good, the bad, and the ugly, but we need to write *something*."

He's silent and I can see him processing my words. When Luca goes silent- which isn't very often- it means he's thinking and considering all aspects of the other person's point of view. I've known him long enough that sometimes his silence is a good enough answer because that means he's considering it. And if he's considering it, that isn't a no, so I nod my head at him with a triumphant smile on my face. "We'll start tomorrow."

Chapter 18

Giovanna

1. Have you ever decided to stop drinking for a week or so, but only lasted a couple of days?
   Yes.

2. Do you wish that people would stop telling you to stop drinking?
   Yes.

3. Has your drinking caused trouble at home?
   Yes.

I put the piece of paper down and take a deep breath. I don't need some Alcoholic Anonymous book to tell me that I'm an alcoholic because I already know I am. My brother seems to think that I need to start taking this "more seriously", whatever that means by that.

"I found that online," Antonio says. "I thought it would be good for me to give it to you."

"Is it just a self-assessment sort of thing?" I ask, trying to see exactly what he wants me to do with this piece of paper.

He nods his head. "I want you to go through it and see how many questions you answer yes to."

I bite my tongue and look at the piece of paper again. I skim my eyes over the page, reading questions all about if I've had more drinks after everyone else stopped drinking, or if I've asked for extra drinks while everyone else is on their first or second, and all that great, fun stuff. I don't have to read it thoroughly to know that I can answer yes to all these questions.

I look back up at my brother with a blank expression.

"So?" he presses.

"What?"

He shakes his head seriously. "How many times did you say yes out of those twelve questions?"

My leg starts bouncing as I break our eye contact. If I look into his eyes, I will break down and cry. He's always been my rock, urging me to do things that I wouldn't normally do because I'm scared, like leaving home to pursue my dreams. To know that I'm about to disappoint him with my answer, and to know that I've already disappointed him and my family by embarrassing myself with the paparazzi already breaks my heart.

"How many, Giovanna?" he asks, a little softer this time.

"Twelve," I whisper, at least I try to, but my answer seems to get stuck in my throat.

He leans in closer, straining to hear me. "Pardon me?"

I can't help the tear that strolls down my cheek. "Twelve."

"Wow," he breathes, leaning back in his chair. I wish he didn't invite me to his home. I wish he would have just called me so I wouldn't have to sit across from him and see the disappointed look sprawled out plain as day on his face.

"I've been trying to get better," I say, but as the words come out, I start to question myself. Am I doing everything I can possibly do? How hard am I *really* trying here? I'm not at a meeting right now,

I'm sitting across from my brother trying to convince him that I'm not completely gone.

He nods his head. "So, you've heard of Alcoholics Anonymous then?"

Everyone's heard of them, but I haven't actually gone to a meeting. I don't know what's stopping me, and I haven't even been able to explain it to Nancy because I'm honestly embarrassed about it, but I have to tell my brother if there's any hope in salvaging my relationship with my family.

"The thought of going to a meeting scares the hell out of me," I admit.

He scrunches his eyebrows together. "Don't you want to get better, though?"

"Of course, I do, but going to a meeting is a daunting task for me," I explain, at least, I try to explain my feelings. "I've never been to one before, so it's completely new to me and I don't even know where to start or where to find one."

He shakes his head and gives me a cold laugh that makes my arm hair stick straight up. "You're joking, right?"

I shake my head, wondering why he would think I would joke when I just told him something that I haven't even told my therapist about.

"You're an idiot," he says, not able to contain his laughter anymore. He's gasping for air at this point now, it's no longer a small chuckle. "You're a complete idiot and I can't believe I keep trying to defend you. Do you know how many journalists have tried to reach out to our parents and I to ask us questions about you? I would need five hands to even *begin* to count how many people have asked us to speak about Insieme, and yet we always decline the offer because that's a complete invasion of privacy for you, Luca, and Tony. Even if we did say yes to them, we don't know how you are because we barely even heard from you! You've even asked us to stop driving you to therapy." I can see the veins popping out of his neck as he yells at me.

"Antonio-"

"You fell off the face of the earth, you let fame get to your head, and you never reach out to your own parents to tell them that you're *alive*. You want to sit across from me right now and tell me that you're not sober because you're too lazy to do a Google search and find a meeting near you?! Are you serious right now? Sometimes I wonder what happened to you." He shakes his head in frustration.

"You clearly have a drinking problem, Giovanna, even a blind man could see that. When there's resources out there to help you, you don't even want to take advantage of them! Not everyone has access to a chance at sobriety, and you want to pour it down the drain because you can't get over a little *anxiety* about going to a meeting for the first time?"

He's breathing heavily with his nostrils flared out, and he's turned completely red in the face. I'm not sure how or even if I want to respond to him because I'm too scared of him right now, so I remain silent as he carries on.

"You know what you are? Selfish. You are so selfish that it makes me sick to my stomach to know that we're related," he spits out, showing that he's clearly repulsed with me. "I'll tell you right now, we have spent the first sixteen years of your life being best friends, and we may look alike, but the only thing we have in common now is our last name. I would never, *ever* have done what you've done to me. I would have never put money, fame, and glory in front of my own family. I'm starting to question all the conversations we ever had about how much you love Luca or even this family because I don't think you're capable of loving anyone except yourself."

"Please, Antonio." I should apologize, but no words are able to slip past my lips.

"Stop crying, Giovanna, I'm so sick and tired of you being able to get out of conversations because you put on the fake tears. If you want to continue to poison your liver every day and piss your days away drinking yourself to death, then be my guest, I don't care. You're dead to me."

He doesn't mean that. He couldn't possibly mean that. I stare at him with tears in my eyes, trying but failing to fix this mess of mine.

"Just go."

It seems as though I'm paralyzed on the spot, unable to wrap my head around what he just said.

"Just go, Giovanna."

So, I do. I get up and walk out, unable to bring myself to look back at my old life line.

Chapter 19

Giovanna

It's been a crazy few days to say the least. First off, let's start with Luca coming back into my life like that, shall we? I was finally feeling good- I had him back in my life and had started to gain hope that I could actually get sober and turn my life around for the better. Yet within 48 hours, I've also heard the words that I never thought would leave my brother's mouth.

I'm dead to him.

I know I've done a lot of messed up things, and I've done things to my family that I promised I would never do to them, and I hate myself for it, but death? No matter how much I may hate someone, I will never, ever wish death upon them, let alone tell them they're dead to me. It seems too much of a loathing thing to say, something that cannot be taken back. I would never speak those words or even think those thoughts into the universe about my worst enemy, and the fact that my own blood did that to me an hour ago is the very reason why I'm cracking open my third beer can.

I drink because I'm depressed, and I'm depressed because I drink.

Never in my life have I ever felt so guilty to have a bottle in my hand, but here we are. When I was wrapped in Luca's arms, I was positive that I would never drink a drop of alcohol ever again in my life. When he came over, it was the happiest I've been in an extremely long time.

It was the happiest I've been in five years.

So, I thought to myself: *this is it, I can actually get sober*. And sitting in Nancy's office, telling her that I want to do something with this sobriety thing and fight this battle on my own, I had gained a sense of hope that made me feel like a million bucks.

I've blamed a lot of people for my mistakes, always putting the blame on someone else and coming up with excuse after excuse as to why everything seemed to *never* be my fault. Not only have I been called out on it by multiple people, but

I've come to realize it myself and become self-aware.

But tonight, I think I have a valid reason to blame Antonio for the state I'm in right now.

While I see where he's coming from because in a sense, he is right. I did go M.I.A. after winning a Grammy and going completely crazy on stage, and sure, maybe I made a joke out of the Rossi name, but I still made a name for myself. I told myself ever since I was a little girl that my name would be in the bright lights of Hollywood, and I finally did something for myself. Alcoholic or not, talented or not, teenager or not, I made a name for myself when I was only sixteen-years-old.

People can hate me all they want, and I've seen all the articles they've published about me, but I don't really care. I'm still talented and no one can deny that, not even me when my self-esteem is ten feet below the ground.

But death? Everyone, even family, messes up once in a while and will disappoint you. The only person you can truly depend on is yourself and your own expectations. It's a bad habit of mine that I'm trying to talk out with Nancy, but I continually hurt my own feelings by setting my expectations of others way too high.

I scroll through my phone, ignoring the thousands of messages that have appeared in my inboxes and scroll straight to Luca's number. I'm no longer surprised when he picks up on the first ring.

"Gia." I think I hear relief in his voice, but that may just be the beers making me delusional. It usually is.

"Hey," I say, sounding relaxed even though I'm feeling anything but.

"Is everything alright?" he asks.

"Is that Giovanna?" I hear Tony ask in the background. I shoot up in my seat and laugh into the phone.

"Tonnnnnyyyyyyyyy."

"Yeah, it's her," he says to Tony, which makes Tony say hi to me.

"Tony, I miss you," I slur. I think they cover the speaker because there's a muffled sound on their end of the line and I can't make out what the two of them are saying, so I start talking into my phone again. "Hey! It's not nice to talk bad about people behind their back. Why are you guys excluding me?"

For one, simple moment, it's like Insieme is still together and we're a bunch of kids arguing over ice cream flavors. But hearing Luca urging Tony to give him some space because something is wrong, snaps me back to reality.

"Giovanna, how much?" he asks once Tony has shut Luca's bedroom door.

I laugh softly. "How much do I want you here? Oh, *so* bad."

He's silent on the phone, and I almost want to ask him if he's still there, but he starts talking again before I have the chance. "Giovanna, that's not what I meant and you know it. How much have you had to drink?"

"Enough to openly admit that I want you here right now," I say, flirting with him without a lick of shame.

He sighs, or laughs, or scoffs- I can't tell- and I'm not too sure why. I thought he wanted me too? I guess he only wants to see me when it's convenient for him, like after a date he couldn't stand. "I can't just come over there, Gia."

"So let me come to you then," I plead. I don't care how desperate I sound or look, if I want to see the only person who is going to take away my pain, then I'm going to get Luca Fonzo.

"You can't drink and drive," he says matter of factly. I know I'm going to feel ten times worse than I already do in the morning because the guilt is already piling high on top of my chest as I talk to Luca.

"I didn't mean to drink, Luca; I genuinely want to get better."

"Are you still at the same motel?" he asks and I hear him picking up his car keys. I also hear Tony coming back to Luca and telling him that he's going to come see me as well, and he's not waiting for Luca to give him permission.

"Yes."

"I will see you in a few minutes, and Tony wants to tag along, too. Giovanna, please put the bottle down until we get there."

He hangs up before I can even promise him that I'll put the beer away. Even though I didn't verbally promise him, I get up and put my can on the counter and sit back down, making sure to make the love of my life a little less disappointed in me.

Chapter 20

Luca

When Tony and I knock on her door, we aren't greeted by Giovanna. Instead, she shouts, "It's open!" from the inside of her room. Tony glances at me with a concerned look, and I don't blame him. First of all, what if something bad were to happen to Giovanna because she didn't lock her door? Second off, is she too drunk to even get up and open the door for us? It should make me mad, but to tell you the complete truth, I'm tremendously scared to see what kind of state she's in.

On the car ride over here, Tony told me not to lose my cool on Giovanna, and I just shook my head at him. I told him that I wouldn't lose it because I'm not mad at her at all. Despite the fact that she has me wrapped around her little finger and I'm a complete and utter fool for her I know that she has been trying her best. I saw it firsthand the other night, and I also saw how much I want to be with her because I can't stand being in the presence of any other woman. So why would I snap at her? I told myself that I need to be here for her and show patience, I need to be the rock that she's always needed, so I told Tony that I have everything under control.

But as I walk, I realize I've never seen her like this before. I'm still not going to lose it, but I sure as hell don't have anything under control. There are clothes, papers, books, underwear, bottles, empty pizza boxes, and other things I can't make out are sprawled all over her room.

What concerns me the most is the fact that she seems to be in some sort of trance. She's sitting with her legs crossed on the bed, staring at a beer can that is sitting on the countertop.

"Giovanna?" I ask. I don't know why I ask, it's obviously her and she can clearly tell we are here, but she hasn't said anything.

She slowly turns her head towards Tony and I, but her eyes are still peeled on that damn can. Those stupid cans have ruined her life. Well, not just that specific Bud Lite can that she's looking at-

I meant alcohol in general- but you know what I mean.

"Hey," she says, half whispering, half slurring her greeting.

I sit next to her, leaving Tony to stand awkwardly in front of the two of us sitting down on her bed now. I place my hands on her shoulders and she feels like a thousand degrees. Her cheeks are completely red, but I can tell the life is completely flushed out of her eyes.

"What happened?" I ask softly, trying my best to give her a small smile. I'm sure my smile came out more like a grimace, but it's just because I'm concerned for her well-being, and right now she is anything but well.

"I'm so sorry."

I look at Tony for a brief moment, who seems to be studying her with a blank expression on his face. When it comes to how Tony feels about Giovanna, I genuinely have no idea. One day he loves her, one day he hates her, and other days he's choosing her side over mine when I suggest something different. He's truly in the gray area on the Giovanna subject, and I can't say I blame him because I'm partially like that as well. I think the main difference between myself and Tony when it comes to our feelings for Giovanna, I think that Tony is struggling with the idea of whether or not he still loves her and if he wants to let her back into his life with the snap of his fingers. He's questioning whether or not she is worthy of his forgiveness, and he has every right to feel that way.

Me, on the other hand, I know that I love Giovanna. Did it take months after losing the record deal to figure that out? Sure, six months to be exact. I didn't fully admit that my undying love for her was still burning deep inside me until I went on a date with a woman who couldn't even hold a candlestick to Giovanna. I know that I want her to be a part of my life until I take my very last breath, so it's not a question of whether or not I want her back into my life. It's a question of to what extent do I want her back into my life right now. Do I want Insieme back with all the tours and glamor? Or do I simply want to hop on a plane down to Las Vegas and have Elvis marry us? I don't know. Two extremes, but both possible nonetheless.

"It's okay, Gia, just tell me what happened." I hope I sound as nice as I intend to. Tony takes a seat on the couch across from the two of us, leaning on his knees in complete focus.

"My brother," she gasps between tears. I don't know when she started crying, it almost happened in the blink of an eye, but I have the urge to guide her head onto my shoulder. I wrap my arm around her while she sobs onto my shirt.

"What happened between you and Antonio?" Tony asks, speaking for the first time.

She shakes her head in disbelief. "He hates me."

"I'm sure he doesn't *hate* you," I say, finding it hard to believe that he would ever say that to her. Perhaps he called her out on something and she took it as though he hates her, but they've always been so close, so I can't imagine those words ever coming out of Antonio's mouth.

"He told me that I'm dead to him."

I bulge my eyes out at Tony, who is wearing the exact same shocked expression on his face. There's no way Antonio would say that to his sister. That is something Vince would do and has done before, but not Antonio. I've known the Rossi family ever since I came out of my mother's womb, and I know that he certainly would never say that to Giovanna.

"Were those his exact words?" Tony asks softly.

"Word for word," she says dryly.

It hits me that ever since Giovanna lost the deal that I never considered what her family was going through. I know that she wasn't keeping in touch with pretty much anybody when we were touring, especially after we won a Grammy. However, I only knew that because Mary told me, not Giovanna. Up until now, I have always blamed Giovanna for losing touch with her family, but looking at this broken girl laying on my shoulder, I'm starting to wonder if I should have told her to pick up the phone and call her family. I know how terrible it feels to have your own brother hate you, and I should have made sure that Giovanna never experienced that feeling.

"Why did you say that?" Tony pushes, walking on eggshells as he asks.

She sits up a little bit and I take my thumb and wipe her tears away from her cheek.

"Well, he told me he wanted to meet up, and I thought that was great and I was super excited. I got to his place, only for him to shove this stupid piece of paper in my face before I even had the chance to say hello."

She's talking about these papers as if we can read her mind and know exactly what she's talking about. This time, it's me who talks. "What paper?"

She reaches into her pant pocket and pulls out a crumpled piece of white paper. She hands it to me with a shaky hand and I gently take it from her. As I unfold the paper, I have to squint to make out the wrecked words because Gia really shoved this thing into her tiny pocket. I stare at twelve questions, and I realize exactly why Antonio said what he said.

They were arguing about her sobriety.

"Walk us through your conversation step by step."

And so, she does. I want to tell you that I'm surprised, but that's only partially true. I'm shocked and blindsided by the harshness and choice of Antonio's words, but I'm not necessarily surprised that he blew up. I can't even say I blame him because I've been there before.

When you're dealing with someone who struggles with addiction, you originally start out with blindness. You tell yourself that they're just having a good time and they can stop anytime they want. In fact, they have you so convinced that it's normal that you even take them out drinking sometimes. Everything is fine, it's just a part, after all.

Slowly, that blindness starts to morph into worry because you stop drinking and they order another one. Then you look at them and the thought that they might be an alcoholic passes through your mind, but that only leads you to feel guilty for even thinking that in the first place. So, you convince yourself that everything will smooth over and continue to act normal. You go to bars with them, drink with them, and maybe even buy them a drink without them asking sometimes.

Eventually that worrying turns into anger because you start to realize that you were right. You know that they have a serious issue, yet you don't know how to confront them. So, one day, you snap and yell at them. You're tired of slowly watching them drink themselves away, so you scream at the top of your lungs and beg them to stop. That's when the fights happen, breakups happen, and you are left with nothing but sadness when all you were trying to do was save their life.

So, your anger boils and boils until it's a tea kettle that's reached its boiling point. Suddenly, you have no communication with the person you cared about the most. Days, weeks, months pass by and during that time, you get no sleep because you can't help but wonder if they're even still alive or if they're drinking right now. People continually come up to you and ask if you're feeling alright because you look as though you've gone ten rounds with Rocky Balboa.

During that time of zero communication, your anger slowly but surely starts to get lower and lower. Soon enough, your anger is now replaced with a burning longing to know if you can still save them. So, it starts off with a simple text or a short phone call where small talk is shared. Eventually, you realize how much better your life is with them than without them, and you start to feel guilty that you weren't patient enough with them. So you decide to turn a new leaf and put your pride and anger aside, fully prepared to walk hand and hand with them on their journey to sobriety because that's what you do when you are unconditionally in love with someone.

"Luca," Giovanna says, bringing me out of my thoughts, "why would he say that to me? He can be mad, he *should* be mad, but why would he go to such extremes?"

I put a curl behind her ear. "I don't know, Gia, but I'm one hundred percent sure that he didn't mean that literally. He's probably just frustrated, and I mean, he is Italian…"

"And all Italians have anger issues," Tony finishes for me. And yes, we can say that because all three of us come from Italian households.

She gives us a sad laugh, but it's something. I've had Giovanna cry a lot of times in front of me, way too many times to count, and now I'm just trying to make her laugh to try something new, a different approach. I've offered her lots of advice, given her plenty of time to speak, and even exploded on her in the past, but more often than not I knew what to say. But what else can I possibly do other than attempt to bring a smile to her face when her brother tells her she's dead to him?

"Especially us Southern Italians," I add with another laugh of my own. She looks up at me with those big, black olive eyes and my heart breaks for her. She looks terrible with her knotty hair and bloodshot eyes.

"I'm mad at myself," she says, disregarding our jokes.

"Why?"

I don't know if she's able to see me through her tears. "For proving him right. When I left his house, I didn't sign up for Alcoholics Anonymous. I didn't sit and think about my actions. My therapist has even suggested that I start writing in a journal, but I've only done that once or twice. Instead of doing what a normal, mature person would and should have done, I cracked open a beer. I feel terrible about it, but that's the only thing I could do. It didn't feel like me- the actions- it felt like I was out of control and dissociated."

I chose to ignore the sinking of my heart as she says that. I know that she's trying, but that's another thing about her drinking that was tough on me, especially when we were touring. She knew that drinking would be the only thing that would make her feel better, not me. In her eyes, drinking is above me, and in my eyes, nothing comes above Giovanna. That can only lead to heartbreak, I know.

Tony clears his throat and stands up as he starts to pace. "We're going to help you, Giovanna. Stop, don't even try to speak right now," he says when he sees Gia opening her mouth to interrupt him. She nods her head and lets him continue. "Right now, it's ten o'clock at night, so you're going to bed right away. We're going to stay the night, okay? Just to make sure that you don't drink anymore and that you don't do anything stupid. In the morning, we are taking you to a meeting and you're going to sit and be open to it. So, help me, Giovanna, if you walk out of that meeting without even giving it a chance, I swear I will punch you so fast."

A little aggressive, but a good point regardless. I'm surprised he wants to stay the night, but he's absolutely right in saying that we need to keep an eye on her.

Giovanna left us in the dust back in Los Angeles, turning our lives upside down and causing us to fend for ourselves. We lost all communication with her and spent countless days angry at her. No matter how wrong she was, no matter how bad she screwed us over, she needs help and there's no denying that. What kind of people would we be if we left her right now?

I will put my pride, my ego, and my racing thoughts aside, and I will not be satisfied until Giovanna gets her life back on track.

Chapter 21

Tony

Was it an impulsive decision to declare that Luca and I were staying the night without even asking Gia if she was okay with it? Maybe. Will it be worth it? I'm not too sure.

As Luca drives down the highway, I can only hope and pray that this works out. Giovanna has been talking about getting better for so long, and I know that she just needs that little extra push, so that's what we're giving her. At the end of the day, I love her like a sister and I will do everything in my power to see her succeed.

We practically dragged her out of bed this morning and forced her to look alive and got her out the door. She got dressed in jeans and a silk button up top, and I know she doesn't feel good, but at least she looks good. I picked out her outfit for her because I know that when I'm in a cute outfit that makes me look put together, I feel better than when I'm wearing sweatpants and an oversized hoodie.

Giovanna barely muttered good morning to us, and the only thing that's filling the silence in Luca's car right now is Billy Joel's singing voice. After flipping through multiple channels and not finding any good music on the radio, Luca told me to just put my own music on. I thought it would be suitable for the situation to put on "Vienna". I know that whenever I feel anxious, which has been a lot lately, this song cured my anxiety better than any medicine or pill ever does.

I twist myself to look at Giovanna sitting in the back middle seat. She gives me a slight smile, trying to make it seem like she's keeping it together, but her bouncing leg is giving her act away.

"It's okay to be nervous," I say as Billy tells her to slow down because she's doing fine.

"I just don't know what to expect," she responds as she tries to take a deep breath.

"But don't you know that only fools are satisfied," I sing along with Mr. Joel again. Luca shoots me a look to tell me that this is not the time

nor place to be singing one of my favorite songs of all time. "You should be proud of yourself for making it this far already."

She nods her head. "Thanks, T."

"You're welcome," I say as I turn around and look out my window. I see the building come into view as Luca signals into the parking lot. I can feel the seriousness of the situation hit us like a train as Luca turns down the music. He circles around the parking lot until he gets to the front doors of the beige building and pops the lock, putting the car in park.

I put my hand on Giovanna's knee. "Good luck in there, we're going to be right here for you once it's over."

"Thanks, Tony," she says as she puts her hand over my own and gives me a small smile. "Love you."

I smile back at her, but I can't bring myself to say those words back to her. I loved her, I still love her, but I don't feel comfortable saying that back right now. It's just too tender of a situation to be throwing that word around. If that makes me a horrible person to not tell her I love her before her first Alcoholics Anonymous meeting, then so be it.

Luca gets out and opens the door for her, if only to reduce the awkward tension between me and her. He gives her his hand to help her out of the car, but doesn't let her walk far enough so that he can close the door behind her. Part of me wants to think that it's because he wants me to hear the conversation between the two of them, but I know it's probably because he only wants to be as close to Giovanna as possible.

The man went through Giovanna withdrawals for months, and he finally had a taste of her again and now the boy is acting as if he hasn't been fed in ten years. He's so in love it makes me want to puke.

"Remember: you can do this. Tony and I wouldn't have pushed you to come here if we didn't think that you are ready, okay?" Because she is so short, he has to crane his neck all the way down and she has to crane hers all the way up so they can look into each other's eyes.

"Luca," she says, closing her eyes and moving her head to the side to avoid eye contact.

"Giovanna."

There are no words being exchanged between them so I put two and two together. It doesn't take a rocket scientist to know that they're lips are all over each other right now. Gross.

"I love you, Luca," she whispers. Now, I can excuse making out in public. Well, ish. But this one, this really catches my breath and surprises me. It was one thing for her to say it to me- I wasn't the one sleeping over last night and it was a "love you" in a friendship way- but I wasn't expecting her to say it to Luca. More importantly, I ain't got a clue in hell as to what Luca is going to respond to this.

I know he loves her, but I also know how much he sees how fragile their situation is right now, and I don't know how far he's willing to push the boundaries.

There's a long, excruciating pause before I hear, "I love you, too, Giovanna." It's almost as though he mutters it, but it is there and out in the open now.

I can't help but have my eyes pop out. I didn't want this to happen because today was supposed to be all about Giovanna and supporting her. I didn't want to distract myself with the drama of their relationship, but damn it, I am intrigued. I love the free content they are handing out to me and I am always down to eat up the drama.

"You're going to do great in there, Gia."

Where is my bowl of popcorn?

"See you in a little bit," she says as he gives her another kiss on the cheek. She walks off and opens the door without looking behind her, but I can tell she's uncertain. Not uncertain actually, just scared.

Luca gets back into the car and I give him a smirk. "Don't," he grumbles.

Oh, but how can I not? We have a full hour before Giovanna gets back into the car.

Chapter 22

Giovanna

I don't want to be here one bit. This place feels stuffy and compact and it smells like old coffee and stale donuts. I should not be here; I should be talking to my hairdresser moments before singing for an audience. Insieme should still be on tour and I should not even be in this rehab facility.

As I walk further in, it seems like everyone is already sitting down in a circle on folding chairs and all eyes land on me. It didn't even cross my mind, but now I wish I had left my motel with a ball cap and hoodie on. Tony forced me to look presentable today in hopes that it would make me feel better, but I'm not too sure this was a good choice.

I take a look around, wondering if I should help myself to the coffee to find something to do with my hands so I don't look as awkward and out of place as I feel, but I think twice about it. I've never been here before and I don't know if it's proper to get coffee before or after a meeting, and I don't even like coffee anyways. I walk to the circle and head over to the only empty chair available. I give a polite smile to the lady who doesn't look a day over thirty next to me as I take a seat and she gives me a great big smile that is a little bit concerning. I wonder why someone would be so happy to be here.

"Good morning, everyone!" a man says, who I assume is the meeting leader.

He gives us the rehearsed spiel about what their mission here is at A.A. and how they want to help us. He assures everyone in the room that there is no judgment from anyone, and he asks that we share our stories truthfully so we can be helped.

To be quite honest with you, I have to stop myself from rolling my eyes at him. There is no way in hell that I'm going to share my testimony with these strangers. Not only would it be embarrassing and humbling to say just how bad of a person I really am when I drink out loud, but I would be handing out free blackmail. Sure, this man- who hasn't even told us his name- is telling us that they're not here to judge, they're just here to help, but what if someone here is a journalist? Or they recognize me already and are going to tell the press that I'm here in hopes to gain some fame of their own. It would bring more shame and embarrassment to my name, not that it hasn't been dragged through the mud already, but I can't do it.

He asks us to pick up the small blue book sitting on the floor to the right of our chairs and everyone does so. Here, we can find the rules and purpose, steps and procedures, and contact information for ourselves to take home with us. It looks way too specific to the piece of paper Antonio handed me and it makes the hairs on the back of my neck stand up as I think back to my brother's words. It's a strong reminder of why I'm sitting in this cold steel chair. I take a deep breath, trying to calm down my overthinking so I can stay here for my family.

"So, let's get straight to the testimonies now, shall I?" he asks, looking around eagerly at each and every one of our faces.

Maybe it's just in my head, but when he makes eye contact with me, it's as though he pauses. He recognizes me, I swear. His gaze, though it was meant to be endearing, makes me shrink in my seat and want to fall off the face of the earth.

"Who would like to start?" he asks, staring directly at me. I look back at him, hoping that he can see the panic in my eyes and that he won't force me to speak.

"I'll go, Daniel," a man who has salt and pepper hair says. He sits up straight in his chair, preparing himself to share his whole life story with the group.

"Hi, I'm Thomas."

"Hi, Thomas," everyone but me responds. I didn't know that was an actual thing, I always thought that was the kind of stuff you only see in movies, but I was wrong.

"Thank you." He takes a deep breath before he gives us his testimony. I sneak a side glance to the nice lady sitting next to me and she has all her attention on Thomas.

"I started drinking at a young age, you know, at first for fun. My buddies and I would get together on a Friday night and we would get so messed up that we couldn't remember what happened the following morning. It was awesome, spending time with my friends and partying without giving a damn about what I did.

"As time went on though, my friends started to settle down. They got married, and heaven knows every man's life ends as soon as he puts a ring on it. They have kids, some of them popping kids out of the oven like they own a bakery." He gets a small laugh from everyone, myself joining in. He seems like a great guy and I'm curious to know about his story, and I'm already in awe that he's brave enough to even speak to the whole group.

"I met a lady, believe it or not, and we started going out. Now, keep in mind that at this point I was thirty-two and still wanted to put my dancing shoes on and hit the club, so settling down was all new to me. I've had a few small relationships here or there, but nothing to the extent

I had with my now ex-wife." Everyone's smile drops from their face and I'm sure I'm not the only one who has to stop themselves from getting up and hugging him.

"We got married after knowing each other for a year; a little bit rushed if you asked me, but she gave me one of those ultimatums. We were married for three years before she finally gave me the boot. Thank goodness there were no kids involved because that would have made our fights and separation even worse." *How is he not crying?* I think to myself as I swallow back threatening tears.

"Every night I would have a drink and she would tell me that I'm drinking too much, which would lead to me raising my voice and telling her to mind her own business. Sometimes I would suggest we go out for dinner and she would always have to drive home because I was too drunk and could barely walk out the door, let alone get behind a wheel. It was four years of constantly hearing her nag at me for everything, and it had always been like that since the very beginning." He pauses for a moment, wiping his eyes with the back of his palm. I feel the lady sitting next to me staring at me as if she's trying to gauge my reaction, and I look back at her. She gives me a slight shrug of the shoulders as if to say "that's life" and then returns her gaze and attention back to Thomas.

"I would drink myself stupid every night, trying to understand how I got into such a shit show of a marriage, and honestly, drinking was an escape for me. It seems like my drinking ended up being my way out of my dead-end marriage. I feel guilty saying it sometimes, and though I wish I wasn't an alcoholic, I know that it was almost like a blessing in disguise."

Blessing in disguise?

"Sure, Jane probably loved me at some point and had I gotten sober earlier, we may have still been together. Yet I know what a life partner should and should not be, and we were simply not meant to be together. We tried for so long, and probably could have tried a bit harder, but I don't think there was a way to fix what we had. Now I'm freshly divorced and trying to get my life together. I'm not even sure if choosing sobriety is the right option, seeing as though I've only been able to stay sober for two months, but it's the best I've felt in years. I think I feel better because I don't feel terrible about drinking as often, but I also know it's because I'm no longer with a person who never supported me."

He goes on to talk about his marriage and how toxic it was in greater detail, but my attention is no longer on him. I'm fixated on the fact that he said his drinking was a blessing in disguise. I don't think anyone gets married for divorce- no one willingly stands at the altar knowing that they are going to fall out of love in a few years- but I'm intrigued with his choice of words.

I can't get over the fact that he called his drinking his blessing in disguise; it's boggling my mind. I've never once thought about my drinking as a blessing. I've only seen it as a curse and wished with every last part of me that I didn't have a drink in my hand, yet I can never put it down. My drinking has become this endless cycle of grief that I want so desperately to break, and as I sit here and listen to Thomas, I can only hope that A.A. can break the cycle.

Maybe I'm too early in my journey to realize that my drinking could have saved me from something, but I can't help but notice that my drinking has only ruined every good thing in my life. In fact, I can't relate to Thomas at all because I don't see how my drinking can ever be a blessing because it's never been in the past.

Once Thomas is finished with his story, he is given a round of applause. Daniel looks at me again when he asks if anyone else would like to share their story, and once again, I shrink into my seat.

The room is painfully silent- so silent that you could hear a pin drop- and the nice lady sitting next to me turns to me again. Now Daniel and this woman are staring at me with anticipation, though I'm sorry to greatly disappoint them. There's just no way I'm sharing my testimony on my first meeting.

I have nothing to share anyways, I'm not even a day sober.

It's as though everyone is able to recognize that two people now have their attention turned to me, so they take it as an invitation to stare at me as well.

I can't share and I won't share. Simple as that.

"There is nothing to be scared about," Daniel says reassuringly, never breaking eye contact with me.

I can feel my heart p

u

m

p

blood and beat, b e a t, b e a t in my chest, sending a blush to my cheeks. I feel my lungs close in on themselves, as though someone has wrapped a wire around my neck and is tightening it by the second.

But when everyone is looking at me as if I'm the latest and greatest thing, how can I turn them down? I've already let everyone down in my life, and I can't seem to fathom the thought that I'll disappoint all these curious eyes.

So, I sit up.

Chapter 22

Giovanna

"I'll go."

That wasn't me. That was some person trying to be the strong version of Giovanna Rossi because there's no way those three words just came out of my mouth. I find that very hard to believe. Maybe it was peer pressure, or maybe it was Daniel's eyes burning straight into my soul, but I said what I said and now there's no turning back.

"My name is Giovanna."

"Hello, Giovanna." The response makes me smile just a little bit. I'm making a complete and utter fool of myself and I can feel my whole body burning. I want to hide away from the world forever, but worse than that, I have the urge to drink right now.

I'm craving to have a drop of alcohol deep down in my bones and I can feel it in my very care. I try to push the thought to the back of my mind, but it's screaming at me. My mind's yelling at me,

"HAVE A DRINK" and there's nothing I can do to muffle it.

"This is my first meeting, so I'm not really sure what to say," I admit truthfully, looking at Daniel to see if he can offer me some advice.

He gives me a warm smile and says, "I'm glad you're here, Giovanna." there's something about him- the way he's looking at me and articulating his words- but I can't quite put my finger on it. He's probably just a fan of Insieme and recognizes me right away, and he's probably not saying anything in front of everyone, which I appreciate.

I nod my head and swallow before I continue. "Thanks," I peep. I want to cry because I feel like everyone can see just how awkward and out of place I am and their smiles are slowly starting to fade. "I basically lost everything because of my drinking. I lost my boyfriend, my career, my friends, and my family."

That's all I want to say right now because I'm not too sure if I want to reveal who I am to the group just yet. Maybe in future meetings, but it seems a little soon to tell them all of my business. "I decided to come here today because I want to get my life back. My *real* life back. I know that I have a drinking problem because once I start, I can't stop. I've tried to get sober by telling myself that I would stop drinking tomorrow, but a drink was in my hand by tomorrow. Every time I wake up and tell myself that today is going to be the day that I won't have a drink, the night time comes along and I'm wasted. It's frustrating, I'm frustrated, and so I thought I would give these meetings a shot. I genuinely have nothing to lose."

Daniel gives me an encouraging nod as I slouch back in my chair. I know my testimony wasn't nearly as good or as long as Thomas's, but it feels good to get that off my chest. It also feels good not to feel like I'm in the shadows of the meeting anymore.

For the rest of the meeting, we go around the circle and tell people about how our sobriety journey is going right now. Daniel makes it clear that you absolutely do not have to share if you aren't comfortable, and again, he looks directly at me when he says that so I take that as a sign that I shouldn't share any more than I have today. Maybe my testimony was triggering for others and he doesn't want me to speak anymore to the group.

So, I sit and listen to everyone share a little bit about their journey's, soaking in all their information like a sponge. After what feels like an hour, Daniel looks at his watch and clears his throat.

"Great job today, everyone. I hope to see you all here next weekend, please remember to stay safe and be kind to yourself." Some people can't get out of their seats fast enough, but I take my time. I turn to the lady next to me, who is gathering her purse and I see no harm in talking to her. However, I'm extremely awkward today and I don't know how to start the conversation with a simple hello and I can't necessarily tell her my name because she already heard my story.

"I love your purse," I say, eyeing her plain black handbag.

A small giggle escapes her lips. "Oh, why, thank you. It's very nice to meet you, Giovanna. My name is Willow." She extends her right hand out for me to shake. Her handshake is firm and bubbly, making me feel a little more at ease.

"It's very nice to meet you, too," I respond, a smile breaking onto my face.

"I got to run to work, but I'll see you next week? Maybe we can grab a coffee or something sometime?" she asks and I'm honestly shocked by her offer.

"That would be lovely, I'll see you then, Willow." And just like everyone else, she dashes out of the building. I take a look around, trying to pinpoint Thomas in the crowd to ask him more about his story. I don't know what's considered rude or not in this situation, but I'm so intrigued about his blessing in disguise comment that I want to find him.

Except when I take a look around me I see that the only other person left in the room is Daniel.

I catch him openly staring at me and I give an awkward chuckle.

"I'm so glad you found Alcoholics Anonymous," he says as he walks closer to me.

"It's been a long, hard journey, believe me."

He ducks his head down and smiles. "I know."

I squint my eyes at him, wondering if he's really a fan or if I know him from some place. Does he say that to everyone who passes through this program, or is he trying to tell me something?

"I'm sorry my testimony was kind of short today."

He waves a dismissive hand in the air. "No, no, please don't apologize. It was very brave of you to share on your first meeting, I thought, as a matter of fact." Is he blushing? "Besides, I respect that you don't want everyone to know who you are right away."

"What do you mean?" I ask, my heart rate shooting through the roof by the millisecond.

He shrugs his shoulders. "I thought I recognized you when you walked in, and then when you said your name, I knew that I had been right."

"Oh," I say, a wave of relief washing over me, "so you know Insieme."

"I know Insieme, yes," he says, but he opens his mouth as if he wants to say more. He opens and closes his lips multiple times before he asks, "You don't recognize me, do you?"

I cock my head to the side and squint my eyes at him again. "Did I sign something for you?"

He shakes his head and averts his eyes to the ground. "No, Giovanna, you didn't sign anything for me."

I stare at him with a blank expression, trying to remember where I've seen his face before. It just goes to show how bad my drinking has gotten if I can't even remember a person's face anymore.

"I'll help you out," he finally utters.

"Please do. I'm so sorry."

"It's me, Danny."

Oh shit.

Chapter 24

Luca

Tony has talked my ear off for a full hour, asking me all sorts of questions about what kind of human being I am. He thinks that making out in public should be a crime and people should get sued for it. I told him it was a little dramatic to say, and he told me that nothing else is new.

"Okay, I don't want to talk to you about this anymore," I announce, clapping my hands together in hopes that he will shut up.

"Oh no, I did not stay up for hours on end multiple times when you were ranting about Gia just for you to silence me now," he claps back, re-adjusting himself in his seat.

I press skip on a song that comes on and Tony looks personally attacked by that action, so I hit rewind so we can hear Drake sing about how he wants to find our love. That's when I notice the clock and see that it's been more than an hour since Giovanna's meeting started.

"I thought I saw some people leave," Tony says, following my eyes and noticing the time as well.

"She should have been out by now." I can only hope that once she gets in this car, Tony will actually shut his trap. I love the guy, I really do, but the man will not leave me alone and it's been an hour straight of nonstop yapping from him. I've barely gotten a word in edgewise.

"Maybe she's talking to someone," he suggests.

I shrug my shoulders. "I don't know, she'll come out when she's ready, I guess."

I know Gia was super nervous to go to this meeting, and she's honestly reminding me of a kid whose parents told them to go take a bath. They never want to get in, but once they are in, they never want to come back out.

"How do you think it went for her?"

"Good, I hope," I say, but those three words don't even hold a fraction of what I want to say.

I am overwhelmed with joy to even be sitting in this parking lot right now because I honestly thought this day would never come. I thought I might have lost her forever, but my hope has been restored. I feel like a proud parent watching their kid score the game winning layup in their first school basketball game.

I don't really know why I keep using all these kid analogies- maybe now that Giovanna is back in my life, I'm starting to recognize that I *am* getting older. Having kids is always something that I've considered. Two would be ideal, a boy first and then a girl, but whatever I'm blessed with, I'm cool with. When I bought the ring for Giovanna, I knew that eventually we would start a family, even though we've never talked about it. It's just sort of a known fact in the sense that if we were going to get married, children would eventually happen.

I always thought that Giovanna was great with kids, hence why she was a dance instructor, so inevitably, she would be a great mom. But then her drinking got worse and it made me second guess myself. I had full intentions of marrying her, but that's when I started to question our future in the children department. Do I think that Samantha and Reen were wrong when they told us that we couldn't get married? One hundred percent; there's no question about that.

Yet it gave me some time to think things through. Sometimes you become so comfortable in a position that it becomes insanity. Giovanna and I had been together for years that everything- no matter how concerning- started to become normal. Samantha allowed us time to separate and grow individually, even though what she did was wrong.

The fact that Giovanna is sitting in a meeting right now and probably striking up a conversation with someone goes to show that things will get better. When Insieme was no longer together, I saw no light at the end of the tunnel. I thought that my life was over and I'd just get stuck working at a dead-end job because I had no other options.

But here I am, sitting in the car with my best friend who is bothering me about my love life. I am patiently waiting for the love of my life to walk out of those doors and thank me profusely for how much I've helped her. Most importantly, Giovanna is going to get her life back. When she gets her life back, I get her back, and then I get to put the ring sitting in the bottom of my drawer on her left hand.

Chapter 25

Giovanna

As usual, I become hyper aware of every single movement of mine and realize how awkward my hands are. I don't know if I should hug him, pat him on the shoulder, or just stand here with my hands balled into fists that are dangling from my sides. Even though I am freaking out because I was not expecting this and I am completely embarrassed that I did not recognize him, I try to sound as nice as possible.

"Oh, my goodness! How have things been?" I ask with a big smile on my face. What's concerning to me is that this is the first big smile I haven't had to fake today.

"I've been great, actually," he says. I'm waiting for him to ask me how I'm doing, but he never does. It might have been an insensitive question anyways, seeing as though I'm in a rehab meeting.

"That's great," I reply. "It's so good to see you, Danny. You grew out your hair; I didn't recognize you." His once short curly hair is now grown out in a small mullet configuration. It's not one of those mullets that is greasy and unkept, it's clean, curly, and suits him like a glove.

"Good to see you too, Giovanna. I am so glad you're here."

At the meeting or back home? I want to ask, but I would only embarrass myself further. Instead, I ask something that I probably should have thought twice about before asking.

"How did you end up with this job?"

He's silent, I'm silent, the whole room is silent. He stares at me, his smile fading and his jaw setting. Maybe I upset him and it sounded like I was talking down to him, but I'm just curious as to why out of all the places we could have bumped into each other that it just so happened to be at an Alcoholics Anonymous meeting.

He turns around and sits back down, and I'm not really sure if he wants me to follow him, but I do anyway and take a seat next to him.

He looks at me, I look at him, the both of us remaining frozen. Except I don't know how to interact normally with others today it seems, so I start laughing because the silence is way too awkward for my liking.

"What's so funny?" he asks between small laughs of his own.

I shrug my shoulders and keep laughing. "I just don't know what to say."

"It's a little bit weird, isn't it?"

It shouldn't be though. I'm making it awkward because I can't keep my eyes off of him. He's aged like fine wine, and I genuinely can't wrap my head around the fact that he's actually here.

"Seriously though, what are you doing here?" I ask again, my curiosity getting the best of me.

He lifts his shoulders up and down. "Do you want the bullshit answer that I give everyone, or the real answer?"

I smile at him. "Both."

"Well, when I told everyone that I was going to become a counselor here after completing my four-year university degree, I got a lot of strange looks. Rightfully so, I guess, because it isn't a common job, especially since I had just completed my Bachelor of Business Administration degree. I told people that I wanted to help people, simple as that."

I nod my head. "Wouldn't it have helped if you had gotten a Psychology or Communications degree if this was the field you wanted to get into?" I don't know where the hell all these questions are coming from and why I can't seem to bite my tongue today.

"My mother pushed me to go into the Business programs," he comments matter of factly. From the little time Danny and I spent together, I remember how much of an unpleasant person his mom was, so it doesn't surprise me one bit that she forced him to do something he wasn't keen on. "When I told people I wanted to help those in need, they kind of brushed it off because I've always been a 'caring person'."

I look into his eyes as I process what he's saying. "So that's the bullshit reason?" He nods his head and smiles, twisting his chest towards me. "So, then what's the real reason?" I press.

"You."

"Excuse me?" I blurt, slapping my hand to my mouth immediately after. "Sorry, that was rude. What do you mean that I'm the real reason?"

He takes a deep breath. "I have nothing personal against you, Gia, so please don't take this the wrong way because I just want to tell someone the truth." I gulp back some anxiety as I nod for him to carry on. "It's just that I saw how much of a terrible person alcohol made you. I saw how it affected you- your thoughts, actions, and emotions- and that was so complicated for me to wrap my head around when I was only 16. I wouldn't say we necessarily dated, but we had something going on and I'm honestly glad I got out of it when I did. Not that I didn't like you, I just didn't like who you were when alcohol touched your system and I just knew."

He pauses for a moment as if it pains him to say what he's about to say, and I can feel my heart rattling against my rib cage. "I just knew that you were going to be an alcoholic. I knew the very moment that you announced you got signed that you're drinking wasn't going to improve anytime soon, and the thought that you were just going to up and leave without getting the help that you so clearly needed made me sick to my stomach.

"I know it's stupid, but for a while, I never forgave myself. I kept telling myself that I should have done more to help you. What made me even more upset is that your alcoholic ways started to become almost glorified in the media. Everyone thought it was so aesthetic how you acted- the drinking, the partying, and the occasional cigarette- but it just made me mad. From the very beginning, you showed clear signs of alcohol abuse and it frustrated me that the media couldn't see that you were crying out for help."

"You knew I was crying out for help?" I ask, my voice barely a whisper.

"Of course, Giovanna, I always knew."

I don't know when I started crying, but the tears have started and they won't stop. I hate that he's seen the worse sides of me, but what's even worse is that he doesn't hate me. He's seen me at my lowest, knew that I needed help but didn't have a way of contacting me, and yet he still wanted to help me.

"A lot of people wanted me to go to rehab," I admit truthfully because I need him to know that there were people close to me who wanted to help, "but I refused. I'm here because I lost my deal and I've been living in a motel for months, Danny. I have to get better and I'm so glad that I have you to help me along the way."

"In training, they told me to treat every patient equally and give the same amount of attention to everyone. No one trained me for the day that Giovanna Rossi would walk into one of my meetings, though, and rock my world for the second time in my life. I'm always going to be here for you, Gia, so please contact me directly if you need anything. I don't care how late it is, how stupid you may think you sound, just call me." He hands me a business card from his wallet and the skip of my heartbeat does not go unnoticed.

"Thank you, Danny. I'm sorry, by the way, for how I acted."

"It's not your fault, Gia. You are sick. I need to get going now, but I suggest downloading a sobriety tracker before our next meeting."

Sick. I almost want to laugh. Being sick doesn't give you an excuse to disrespect pure people like Danny who are too nice for this world and treat them like garbage.

Chapter 26

Giovanna

When I get into the car, the boys are way too quiet when I saw them clearly moving their mouths when I was walking out, so they must have been talking about me. I'm not surprised because I expected them to since they've been wanting me to go to one of these meetings for years.

I don't say anything when I get in, though, because I have no idea if I should mention Danny. Honestly, I wish they would have just dropped me off and left because this is one of those moments where I don't want to be around anyone, like after a session with Nancy. All I want is to lay in bed all day and reflect on my feelings. I want to go to my appointment with Nancy tomorrow and tell her everything that just happened and exactly how I'm feeling. That's all I want.

I don't want to be in this car where the heat's pumping from the fans and Tony's blaring music, and I actually have to act as if I'm keeping it together. As if I'm okay.

Luca starts driving, catching my eyes in his rearview mirror every now and then instead of keeping his eyes on the road. I know how bad of a person it makes me that I'm not talking to them after they've been wasting their morning here with me.

I clear my throat, realizing that they're waiting for me to be the first one to speak. "I'm glad I went."

Tony looks at Luca before he looks back at me. I can't read Luca's face in the mirror, but I can see his jaw unclench a little bit.

"That's good," Tony says. I can tell that he has so many questions, but I know he sees that I have absolutely no answers for him this time.

"There's a meeting at the same time and place next week," I say.

"Yeah?" Luca asks as he accelerates to merge.

"Yeah. I was talking to the counselor a little bit after the meeting was over and he told me about this sobriety tracker app that I can download onto my phone. It'll send me daily reminders, and I can even program it into hourly reminders I think, and he said it would help me while I wait for the next meeting."

"That sounds great, Gia," Luca says, interrupting me mid-sentence.

"I thought there were always meetings going on, though?" Tony asks.

"Well, technically there are, but…"

"You should go tomorrow," Luca says, interrupting me mid-sentence.

I shake my head. "I want to go next week."

"Maybe we should consider going once every week when you have been sober for a longer time, *amore*. You should get as much help as you can now."

I know he did not just *amore* me right now.

"Going every day is going to be too much for me, Luca."

"You can't get sober if the meetings aren't habitual," he counters.

"You weren't there!" I snap, slamming my hand down on the leather seat and causing both of them to jump. "Okay?! I just need some time to think about this and let it soak in. You weren't in the meeting and didn't have to hear traumatic story after traumatic story, and if you think for one second that I'm going to listen to a bunch of those stories for days in a row, then you are sorely mistaken. Plus, I have a therapist appointment, so I'm not going to be completely alone."

Luca opens his mouth to say something, but Tony stops him. "Whatever you need, Giovanna." And that's the end of the conversation.

I didn't mean to snap at him, but I feel like he gave me a good reason to. I know he means well, but I just couldn't handle his ignorance. That's why the rest of the car ride was spent in silence with the music turned so low that you had to strain to hear it.

When we get back to the motel, I feel like I should thank them for everything, so I clear my throat and prepare myself to talk again. "Thank you for taking me today. I couldn't have done it without you." And that's the truth. If they hadn't showed up, I probably would have had six beers and been extremely hungover right now, so they did save me last night.

"No worries. Get some rest," Luca says in a harsh tone. I can tell that I've hurt him and he's probably just as confused as I am, but I'm honestly too tired to think of ways to fix our problems right now.

"See you," Tony responds with a little wave. I pull on my door handle and let myself out, not bothering to look back and wave goodbye as Luca drives off. For now, I need some sleep.

When I wake up, I roll over and see that it is three o'clock in the afternoon, and my whole body is covered in damp sweat. I rub my eyes and sit up, clutching my teddy bear.

I pick up my phone and see that Luca has texted me and asked how I'm holding up two hours ago. I will respond to him eventually, but what I really need right now is to take a step back from my phone and take a hot shower.

I get up and run myself a hot shower while I listen to my CD player. I know my music career has almost been the death of me, but music has also saved me in a way that I don't think anyone or anything will ever be able to. Putting on my favorite songs is like a way for me to travel to another dimension. The music and lyrics just scratch my brain in a certain way that always seems to fix me.

Once I'm out of the shower, I put on a pair of sweatpants and a cozy sweater, feeling great in my freshly shaved skin. I think about my day today and how productive and crazy it was. It's honestly a lot for me to process by myself, so I can't wait for my session with Nancy tomorrow. I know she will have a lot to say about everything I'll tell her, but I also know she's going to be extremely proud of the fact that I finally got into a meeting.

I consider picking up the phone and telling Antonio that I got my butt in gear and I'm starting to get sober for real, but I can't bring myself to do it. For tonight, I'm just going to disappear and not touch my phone. I think it's important for everyone to take a step back from social media and regroup ourselves once in a while, focusing only on what is best for us.

So instead of grabbing a glass of wine and scrolling on my phone for hours on end while I wallow in self-pity, I decide to pick up my journal and flip to a new page. I already know that Nancy is going to be pleased with the fact that I went to a meeting, but she is going to be extra proud when I tell her that I went back to my hotel room and wrote about my feelings in my journal.

Besides, I've got an enormous number of feelings bursting at the seams to be free from my mind.

Chapter 27

Giovanna

"It seems like a lot has happened in the past few days. I'm impressed on how well you've been keeping it together," Nancy comments once I'm done explaining how I've been ever since I saw Antonio.

I nod my head. "I would be lying to you if I said it's been easy."

"First off, even getting to the meeting is a huge accomplishment, and you should be so proud with how far you've come."

You know what? I am proud of myself. Considering that my liver was bound to fail any given minute and I had ruined everything, it feels nice to say that I'm at least putting in a real effort to get my life back on track now.

"Now, can we circle back to Antonio?" she asks. I cringe at her question and I can tell she notices it. "I know it's a sensitive subject."

I've come to realize that crying in a therapy session is completely normal, but I was trying to keep it together today to show her I'm better, but I obviously failed.

"He's my brother, of course what he said hurt me," I say through tears. "It shocked me because I've never seen that side of Antonio before. Sure, he's gotten mad about little things here and there, but I've never seen him explode like that. He was like Mount Vesuvius the other day, and I don't know how to talk to him again."

She thinks for a minute before she speaks again. "Have you told him that you went to a meeting?"

"No."

She nods her head slowly, thinking of a solution for me. "Why is that?"

"He told me I'm dead to him," I state.

"Right, but he also said that because you had yet to go to a meeting. What do you think his reaction would be if you were to call him right now and tell him that you went and actually liked it."

"Like is a strong word," I clarify, raising my finger up.

"What do you think his reaction would be if you were to call him right now and tell him that you *attended* a meeting?" she asks again with a small smirk; I can tell she's holding in a laugh.

I shrug my shoulders. "I think, quite honestly, that he would say that it's about damn time that I got my life together."

"Is that the worst-case scenario?"

Again, with the questions. I just want her to tell me what to do. Whenever I start to think we're making progress in our relationship and that she understands me, she goes ahead and asks me questions when all I want is her answers. I want her to tell me how to approach Antonio, or even if I should reach out to him at all.

"I don't know," I say honestly. "I'm too scared to talk to him again, and I genuinely think that I will give him some rightfully earned space and wait until he wants to talk to me. After all, I am the one who fell off the face of the earth, so he does deserve to give me the cold shoulder."

"I see where you're coming from, and it's mature of you to look at it that way," she says, being the first person to call me mature in years, "but I just want to let you know that you didn't deserve that. What he said, I mean, you didn't deserve to be told that."

I swipe away a tear with a tissue and thank her. It does mean a lot, and I know that I have messed up and haven't been a great person, but hearing those reassuring words from Nancy does wonders for me. It reminds me that I can be who I used to be before I let alcohol ruin my life. It also reminds me that there will always be people who understand me and are willing to listen, and that I'm not alone, despite how I feel.

"Is there anything else that should be addressed in more detail? It's your session, so we can talk about whatever you want," she carries on.

I nod my head. "I'm so confused with my love life right now, it's not even funny." I can't help but laugh at how idiotic I sound.

"How so?"

"Danny."

"Right."

My phone buzzes in my pocket, which I only have my family, Luca, and Tony's numbers allowed to notify me when my phone is on do not disturb, so it must be one of them. "Sorry, I need to respond to this," I apologize as I pull out my phone. I see a text from Luca and I don't necessarily get a happy feeling in my chest, nor a sad one, but a weird one.

Luca: Is everything okay? Me and Tony swung by your place to check on you, but no one's answering. Can you open up for us?

The fact that he would even think that I would hear his knock and not open the door makes my heart sink. I text back as quickly as possible so I can get back to my session.

Me: Just at therapy right now… Didn't know you were coming to visit me today. The padlock code is 5830, let yourself in and I should be back within the hour.

I shake my head as I put my phone back in my pocket. "Well, Luca just texted me and told me he's outside my door with Tony."

"You sound annoyed," she points out, crossing her legs.

"I am. I don't know why he would think it's okay to show up to my room out of the blue. I'm not always going to be there- they can't expect me to live there all day, every day- and it aggravates me that he didn't bother to tell me they were coming by."

She nods her head. "It seems as though you're already mad at Luca, or else I don't think you would let this little thing bother you as much as it is, considering he's swung by before."

"It's..." I feel like a terrible person saying what I want to say, but I know Nancy keeps everything confidential.

"It's okay, you can say whatever you need to say," she encourages sincerely.

I take a deep breath and close my eyes. "Danny made me feel things I haven't felt in a really long time."

She keeps a neutral expression. "How so?"

"Him and I have a little history, and it's like a big gray elephant in the room when we're together. I'm not saying that I'm attracted to him or I want to date him- that's not what I mean when I said he makes me feel things. I meant that I feel a sense of calmness when I'm around him. It's as if I'm lying in the middle of the ocean without any wind when he talks to me. He was patient and understanding back when we were sixteen, and he is still showing me a tremendous amount of compassion."

"So, he understands you?"

I nod my head. "I'm hard on myself, and I think it's good to be hard on yourself to a certain degree for accountability, but I also think it's important to surround yourself with people who are there to tell you to back off once in a while. When Danny saw me, he was so overwhelmed with joy that I had finally turned up to a meeting, and he pledged to me that he is going to help me get sober. I'm just saying that he's still being kind to me when I've been nothing but a horrible person to him."

"And?" she asks once I've paused, knowing I have more to say.

"And it's just that, Luca never…"

"You can say whatever you want; I'm not here to judge."

"Luca never showed me that patience. I know I messed up and there's no denying that, but Luca just exploded. He cut off all ties and told me that I need to get my life back together. Even before I lost the record deal, he would yell at me and tell me to grow up. As soon as I lost the deal, though, suddenly he was this all-mighty saint and he claimed he tried to save me, but I wouldn't listen. It's just frustrating."

"And with Danny you feel like he's a little bit more understanding when it comes to drinking."

"Yes, exactly," I say, glad to hear that someone doesn't think I'm crazy. "Luca loves me, but he's only kissing me now because I'm getting better. I wouldn't say that I'm extremely high up, but I'm not the lowest I've been. He wasn't there for me at my lowest. Danny was there for me, and still continues to be there for me, at my lowest. He asks questions, but he asks the right ones that he knows will help me, not just benefit him. It's almost like Luca selfishly wanted me to get better just so his life could get better, if that makes any sense?"

She nods her head. "It does make sense, but I also think you're not giving Luca enough credit. To be fair, he did get into a relationship at a young age with you, and he was probably having a hard time seeing the little kid in you die, if you will."

"I know, and I don't want to discredit Luca at all because I love him, obviously," I say, quickly trying to explain myself.

"It was nice to not be looked at like a monster for once. Danny showed you that you could still be saved, and that's all you ever really wanted," she finishes.

"I couldn't have said it better myself, Nancy."

Chapter 28

Luca

Tony and I completely forgot about Giovanna's therapy session, and now I feel like a total jerk that I bothered her. I have no idea if she's going to be mad at me when she walks in that door, but for now, I'm making myself comfortable. I wouldn't call it snooping, I would call it *observing*.

I sit on the bed where we've shared multiple conversations and reach for the bedside table, pulling the drawer open.

"Do you know how long she's going to be?" Tony calls from the washroom.

"No, take you time," I laugh, knowing he's going to be sitting on his "throne"- as he calls it- for an hour.

When I open the drawer, I see a lavender notebook with the word *Notes* written on it, and I pick it up. It makes me happy to see a songbook because that meansTony and I will have to write less songs.

Believe me when I tell you that I've tried to have an open mind when it comes to songwriting, but Giovanna's just too damn good at it, and I'm just too damn bad at it for it to work.

Except when I open the book, I notice that I'm not looking at songs at all. I should put it down and respect her privacy, but I need to know how she's feeling. If I can know exactly where her head is at right now, it'll be easier for me to help her.

I notice that the first page is from nearly six months ago, talking about how she can't believe Insieme broke up. I skim the pages, but there's not much to note other than she was heartbroken. What piques my interest is the latest journal entry she made yesterday, which seems to be one of three whole entries she's made. I guess she was never able to stick with journaling. I look up again, checking left and right just to make sure I'm alone while I read:

December 9,

I went to my first Alcoholic Anonymous meeting yesterday, and I'm not too sure how to feel.

At first, it felt like everyone was staring at me- as if they recognized me from their Entertainment Tonight! subscriptions. Maybe it was that or maybe it was because I was new, but I honestly felt severely uncomfortable with all of those eyes on me.

What I can't get over is the fact that the counselor was looking at me intensely from the very moment I stepped foot into the building. I thought he was a huge Insieme fan and was mad that we hadn't released anything new, but I was sorely mistaken. I had no idea that the counselor was Danny. As in Danny Garcia from high school. But I didn't find out until after the meeting, so I'll get into that later.

I want to talk about Thomas. Thomas is this forty-year-old who had an amazing testimony. He acknowledged that his drinking is a problem, but he also said it was a blessing in disguise because it allowed him to get out of his "dead end" marriage. I think it was interesting of him to take on that perspective- that his drinking is a blessing. For as long as I can remember, my drinking has only wreaked havoc on me and those that I love the most, so I had to take a step back when he shared that with everyone in the meeting.

Can my drinking be a blessing in disguise? If so, what would it possibly be? All I know is that I worked my ass off all day every day since I woke up from my dream and I was constantly trying to prove to everyone that I could be a singer, only for me to watch everything come crumbling down because of my drinking. So, I don't think there's a blessing in disguise here, but I'm sure Nancy and I can talk through that at some point.

Danny. Danny, Danny, Danny. You know what's scary? Is that he made my heart skip a beat. I don't want him to and I know it's wrong of me, but I actually felt the happiest I've felt in a really long time because of him. At first, I was completely embarrassed and utterly ashamed that Danny was the counselor, but as we started to talk more after our meeting, I was oddly comforted by his presence. The whole world seems to have their own idea about me, and my relationship with Luca and Tony is too unstable to rely on right now, so talking with Danny was refreshing.

There was no drama, no harsh feelings, no awkwardness other than at the beginning when I told him that I had no idea who he was. Lately, I've been feeling on edge. Whether it's around my family, Luca and Tony, or even just walking out onto the street with the fear that I'll be pestered by the paparazzi, I just feel like I'm constantly walking on eggshells. But with Danny, I could just simply be. I didn't have to watch what I said, I didn't have to worry if I was offending anyone, and he is the first person that made me feel normal. He makes me feel fixable and not like some sort of monster who makes it their personal vendetta to ruin other people's lives.

What scares me the most is that when I got into Luca's car, I felt annoyed with him. I was so upset that he wanted me to go to another meeting as if these are easy to go to. He showed no patience whatsoever, and it just made me realize how great of a person and counselor Danny is. But as soon as that thought crossed my mind, I was sick to my stomach with guilt. The only reason I was there in the first place was because Luca and Tony dropped everything just to take me to the meeting.

I'm just confused right now. I don't like Danny as more than a comforting old friend, but it made me realize that maybe Luca and I aren't as great of a match as I hoped we were. Maybe we've been together for so long that we have no idea how to be apart now, but maybe- just maybe- we aren't meant to be forever. Forever isn't for everyone, after all.

I slam the book shut and pace the room, reaching for my hair and pulling on it. If I can make myself physically hurt, then maybe the aching in my chest will stop.

"Is everything alright?" Tony asks, emerging out of the washroom.

I look at him and then back at the cursed journal I was just reading, and then back at my best friend. "It was him."

Tony looks at me with furrowed eyebrows. "What was him?"

"Danny," I say, disgusted to even have his name on my tongue.

"Excuse me?" he asks. "Do you speak English anymore?" Tony lets out a little laugh, but there's nothing funny about this situation.

I nod my head to the journal sitting on the bed. "I accidentally found her journal. You're going to want to read this."

"I don't think we should be reading that, Luca."

"Just do it, T. I already did. I know I probably shouldn't have, and I wish I didn't, but I did and now I can't unread what the hell I just saw. Please, I don't even want to repeat what I read out loud so, please, just read it."

He puts both hands up. "Sounds like I don't have much of a choice." He sits down on the bed and picks up the book.

"Just read the last one."

He nods his head and I stay quiet so he can read in silence. The only sound that fills this stuffy, stupid room are the tears that I'm trying to sniff back. But how can I possibly stop the tears when my heart is s

i

n

k

i

n

g?

Chapter 29

Tony

My heart jumps out of my chest and I
literally chuck the journal across the room when the
door flings open and Giovanna walks in. She stares
at me and Luca with her mouth open as her eyes
wander all around the room and land on her journal
lying on the ground. I feel extremely guilty that I
read her personal thoughts; it was a complete
invasion of privacy.

"I didn't know you guys were coming over,"
she says calmly, her voice barely a whisper as she
picks up her journal.

"It was kind of a spur of the moment type of
decision," I reply, trying to act natural as if we
didn't get caught red-handed.

She nods her head as she sets her lips into a
hard line. "I had to pause my therapy session to text
you back," she continues, not looking at Luca as she
talks to him. I feel awkward, awful, and completely
in the wrong as I look back at Giovanna.

But, seriously, Danny? I didn't see this coming. It's crazy how you just reconnect with people from your past in the most peculiar ways. Sometimes when I'm working, someone from my high school will walk in and I'll end up being their waiter, so it's not impossible to bump into familiar faces now and then. Though I am interested in knowing how exactly Danny ended up with that kind of job.

"We forgot about your appointment, I'm sorry," I respond for Luca because he seems to be a statue frozen on the post. He's fuming, I can feel it, and I know that this is simply the calm before the storm.

"I told Nancy that I would respond quickly so we could get back to our session. I was trying to get back to the session that I paid for, I wasn't thinking and just automatically gave you the code to get in."

She pauses, walking slowly and deliberately as she places her journal back to its original spot. "How silly of me to trust you alone in my makeshift home." Now, she looks at Luca. "For a dumb minute, I automatically thought we were all good, and I could trust you again."

He gives her a cold snicker, and just that noise sets an alarm off inside of me and it yells at me to stop this immediately. I know that things are about to get really bad, real fast. Yet I can't seem to find the courage to speak up, I just remain silent.

"You walk to talk about trust?" I see Luca bite down on his bottom lip, trying to stay as calm as Gia is right now.

She laughs. "Well, I'll tell you this right now. If I showed up to your house uninvited and you let me in, I would watch TV or go on my phone. I wouldn't dig through your personal belongings, and if you just so happened to have a journal and I stumbled upon it, I sure as hell wouldn't go reading through it."

He throws his head back, looking up at the ceiling. "What do you want me to say? I already read everything."

"I want you to get out," she whispers, tears threatening at her voice, nearly exposing her calm, cool, and collected act she's put on.

"I'm not leaving, Giovanna. I'm not going to walk away when it gets hard like you do."

That was uncalled for. "Hey," I say, but it's no use, they've already started to talk over me.

"I didn't walk away when it got hard, you did," Giovanna spits.

"Right, right, and picture-perfect Danny over there didn't walk away, so why don't you go and call him," Luca snarls back.

"Excuse me?"

"Did I stutter?"

Oh boy, here we go again. At this point, I either chose to sit back and observe, or walk straight into the fire and get burned, and I will not be doing the latter today. As intense as this conversation is, it was bound to happen, and who am I to get in the way of destiny?

"When my drinking got even worse, did you ever stop to think that maybe your approach of yelling at me every day wasn't working? You didn't even think to mention that the due date for the album was approaching, but according to everyone in the whole world, you did whatever you could to help me. Here's a news flash: your strategy of slamming the door in my face and making me feel like I've got three heads on my shoulders doesn't work! You can't just pretend like I'm the only bad one in our relationship."

He nods his head slowly. "You see, that's the problem with you."

"Luca, don't-" I warn, but he waves me off with his hand. "I said stop, Luca, you're going to regret this," I say again, ignoring his wishes. I know exactly what he's going to say and I know that in two months- or even better, two hours- he's going to be crying about what he said and ask for advice on how to fix his mess.

"Sure, maybe I should have warned you about one of the biggest dates on the damn calendar that our anticipated album was supposed to drop. Maybe I should have soothed you in a better way if that's what you're looking for me to say. But don't pretend like you're not the common denominator in all of this. If I have an issue, Tony has an issue, Mary has an issue, and your *brother* has an issue with you, maybe it's time to look at who always seems to be involved in the big fights."

She shakes her head. "You're not listening to me. I know how badly I mussed up, and I'm sorry. I take full responsibility for my actions, but I am sick and tired of you sitting on your little high chair, pretending like you're some sort of holy angel that's so pure."

"Dammit, Giovanna!" he screams, causing me to jump up. I forget how loud he can get sometimes. "Giovanna, I love you. I don't know what more you need me to say or do to prove that to you." His voice breaks as tears stream down his hot red cheeks. "I don't know what you're looking for, I don't know how to comfort you and maybe you think Danny is better for you, but he also doesn't know what it's like to have his whole career ruined because of you."

"I never said I wanted to date Danny-"

"And I know that you're going to say that it takes two to tango, and that may be true, but own up to your faults, Giovanna. You can't just keep doing horrible things and expecting everyone to sit back and clap for you. Have I not proven that I love you? I came over after a horrible date, I drove you to a meeting, and I even let you cry on my shirt over Antonio!" He's growing more frustrated by the minute, and I know that there's really nothing I can say or do to bring him back down to the ground.

"I never claimed that you didn't love me," she says, trying to tell her side of the story.

"I dealt with this when we were 16, and I'm not going to deal with it again. If you truly wanted me, you wouldn't have eyes for anyone else, and I only have eyes for you, Giovanna. I can't keep going around in circles and having the same conversations with you. I love you, simple as that. If you don't love me back, just tell me and stop using me and stringing me along."

For the first time in fifteen minutes, it's completely silent in the room. I even find myself sitting on the edge of my seat, waiting for Giovanna's response.

"I don't know," she whispers, clamping her mouth shut.

Luca stares at her in disbelief. "I get it."

He definitely doesn't get it, I can see it in his eyes. His earth has shattered for the second time because of Giovanna, and it's naturally up to me to repair it for him again. I'm not saying that one or the other is completely right in the situation, but I think that's exactly their problem. Their pride in the need to be right and never admit that they are wrong is the root of all their issues, and it's quite toxic.

"I just need time, Luca. I never said I like Danny, but if that's what is in your head, I'm not sure what else I can say to convince you otherwise."

Tell him you love him, I think, but I bite my tongue.

"If you loved me, Gia, you wouldn't need time to think." He nods his head at me and I shoot up from my seat. We walk over to the door and I look back at Gia, wondering if we're right back at square one again.

For one, single day, I thought Insieme could get back together. There was no toxic management involved, no deadlines, and we seemed to be enjoying each other's company. I've always thought that the reason Insieme ultimately failed was because of everyone else- like the pressure fans and management put on us. However, standing here in this tiny room, I realize that the issue all along has been two people who don't know how to communicate.

Chapter 30

Giovanna

As soon as Luca slams the door in my face with Tony close on his heels, I pull out my phone and call Danny.

"Giovanna?"

"I want a drink," I bubble out, my emotions completely taking over me. "I just had a huge fight with Luca, and I don't know what to do because he just walked out on me, and I just really want a drink."

"Okay, okay, slow down," he starts, breathing deeply on the other line. "We can talk through this."

"I don't want to relapse, Danny, but I don't want to feel this pain anymore."

"What's going to be worse, Giovanna, the pain you're feeling now, or the hangover?"

While I do know he has a point because hangovers leave me with nothing but a headache and a guilty conscience, the craving is still burning inside me. "What do I do, Danny?"

He's silent for a few moments, thinking about how to save my life yet again. "Here's what you're going to do: you're going to get off the phone with me and download the app I told you about. You're going to set up a profile for yourself and begin tracking your sober days, and then you're going to shut all your other apps on your phone except the music one. You're going to go for a long walk while listening to your favorite music, but it can't be sad music, Giovanna, that will only make it worse."

"I don't really feel like walking right now, Danny," I say softly.

"I need you to do this for me, Gia. You need something to take your mind off of alcohol, and walking in fresh air is going to help you."

I take a deep breath. "Okay."

"I'm here if you need anything else, Giovanna, and I just want to let you know that I believe in you."

"Thank you, Danny."

"I'll see you at next week's meeting," he says before he ends the call.

As soon as I'm off the phone, I download the sobriety tracker app and set up my profile, selecting the alcohol-free option and choose a purple and blue colored background for my app.

I'm overwhelmed when I see the number of people active on the app and sharing their journeys. The app asks me why I want to get sober and I say that my drinking has ruined everything good in my life. Once they ask me a few more questions about whether or not I've tried to get sober before, how long I want to get sober, and a few inspiring quotes, the sobriety tracker starts.

I've been sober for 36 seconds.

I close out of the app and grab my headphones, put on my shoes, and walk right out the door. Damaging as it may be on my eardrums, I put the volume up all the way as I click on Amy Winehouse's fantastic album, "Back to Black."

I can't help the smile that breaks onto my face when "Rehab" starts playing first as I continue to walk down the street. I have no idea where I'm walking, but I just keep putting one foot in front of the other while the bright sun beats down on me. I'm hit with the memory of Luca and I walking along the beach in California when we first moved out there, and I feel my heart weeping of melancholy as I think back to simpler times.

Amy's angelic voice fills my ears as I think about what just happened. I can go down the rabbit whole of why Luca shouldn't have done what he did, but that helps no one, especially me. The fact of the matter is that I can wish things were different all I want, but it won't change what's happened. Now I have to deal with it because this problem is not going to fix itself.

The fact that Luca would even think it's okay to go through my personal belongings still shocks me, but that's what I've been saying from the very beginning: people will always disappoint you. No matter how close you think you are or how much you think they love you, you are always going to be let down. I am a firm believer that there are only two things we can be certain about in our lifetimes: death and disappointment.

I look up and spot someone clearly taking a photo of me, not even considering hiding their phone. I shoot my head down and avoid eye contact because I'm not in the mood for fans or press today. Right now, I need to make some decisions.

Where do I see myself in five years? Perhaps I'm married to Luca with a few children. Where does that leave me career wise? Am I even capable of having children? That would mean I would have to get sober and I just don't know if anyone will ever trust me to get sober for good. And how will that affect my career? I can't tour with children.

Do I even see myself with Luca? He's all I've ever known. I've known plenty of people and heard lots of stories about how they're happily married to their first partner, but do I know anything else? If I've never experienced a relationship with someone else, how will I know if Luca is the one?

That may make me a bad person for even thinking that, but I somehow don't feel guilty saying it.

I walk for maybe an hour until my feet start to feel like there are nails hammered into them. I take a look around to see exactly where I am, and it seems as though I've unconsciously walked all the way to my uncle's restaurant.

All the memories come flooding back to me as if a dam has broken in a rushing river. As I listen to Amy Winehouse belting in my ears and stare at Pazzo's, I start to reflect on my past.

This all started because I had a dream that I was in Insieme. I could have woken up- trust me that I've wished multiple times that I had just forgotten all about it- and went on with the rest of my life normally. I could have just continued doing the same routine and getting no further ahead in life. I probably would have been in post-secondary education right now, and I guarantee you that I definitely would have my high school diploma.

But that didn't happen. I woke up and willingly chose to seek out Tony and Luca, convinced myself that fate brought us together, and persuaded them to upload a stupid YouTube video. I didn't anticipate that we would blow up overnight, but a big part of me wanted that to happen. When it started blowing up, I thought to myself that I could get used to it. That feeling of excitement that starts in my toes and makes me blush like a little girl is what I want to feel every day for the rest of my life. I guess you could say that the rest is history- the tours, the triumphs, the Grammy, and of course, the downfall.

What goes up, must come down, right?

It was too good to be true and I should have known that, but I can't change the fact that I took the deal. It's not like I can go back in time and decline Samantha's call, so there's only one thing for me to do. I can sit here and sulk and let Luca's words affect me and drag me down. I can walk around the city and think about ways to disappear off the face of the earth, but starting a second life in Italy with a new name is simply impossible.

So, I start to walk back to my room, putting on "Here I Go Again" by Whitesnake on look as I turn around. *I don't know where I'm going// but I sure know where I've been.* As I listen to the lyrics that describe exactly what I'm going through right now, a bright smile breaks onto my face.

There's only one thing left for me to do now. I got to get home and write a song.

Chapter 31

Luca

When we get back home, I'm prepared for a beating of a lifetime from Tony, but he's oddly quiet.

"Everything okay?" I ask.

He shakes his head and scoffs. "Did you seriously just ask me that?"

"Well, you're not saying anything," I point out.

He throws his hands in the air and slams them against his thighs. "What exactly do you want me to say, Luca? I think the two of you guys are acting like immature children who throw hissy fits over the fact that their sibling ate the last piece of chocolate."

"That's valid, but do I not have the right to feel this way?" I ask, trying to get my side of the story out. "Tony, I dropped *everything* for her the other day, just for her to realize that she probably doesn't love me that much now? I feel like I was competing against Danny when we were teenagers and I still feel like it to this very day, and I'm tired of it. I'm done feeling like the second option when I put her on a pedestal.

"She never said you were the second option! First off, you should have *never* read her journal. Once you found it, you should have just left it closed and respected her personal space, but you didn't. You completely invaded her privacy."

"No," I say, interrupting him, "because you know what, T? As soon as I saw that journal, I had a gut feeling that she wasn't telling us something. I had a feeling she was lying to us, so I really don't want to hear all this crap about an invasion of privacy."

"Did she lie, though?" he asks. "Did she really? She got into the car after the meeting and was silent, sure, but she never *lied*, per say. Withheld some truth, maybe, but haven't we all?"

I cock my head to the side and scrunch my eyebrows together. "Why are you taking her side on this?"

"I'm on nobody's side!" he yells, veins popping out of his neck. "I'm sick of choosing between the two of you, especially when you guys would drop me in a heartbeat if you guys were to get back together."

"What?" I blurt, taken aback by his words

"You know exactly what I mean. Whenever you guys get into a fight because apparently communication is hard in this relationship, I always have to side with one or the other. I'm the rebound friend, if we're being honest here. When the two of you guys get back together, you completely forget about me all the time or make me feel like the biggest third wheel known to mankind. If you guys get married, you're not going to want to live with me anymore, you'll move in with her in a heartbeat. You guys only care about me when it happens to be convenient for you."

"That's not what it's like at all. You just don't understand because you've never been in a real relationship before."

As soon as that comment leaves my lips, I want to turn back time. I should not have said that, and I can see that my words have physically hurt him. "Tony, I'm sorry, I didn't mean-"

He's zoned out now, looking at me with clouded, teary eyes. "You think I don't want a relationship? Really, Luca? After everything I've told you? You know I was put in a situation with Reen and you know how my parents are, so why would you say that?" I open my mouth to apologize again, but he keeps talking with the same zoned out expression. "We can say that we had toxic management, but we all know that at the end of the day, Insieme ended because of you, Luca."

He shakes his head, snapping himself out of the trance and then walks out the front door. He leaves me standing in our living room, wondering why I seem to break everything I touch.

Chapter 32

Giovanna

I want to write something that isn't necessarily heartbreaking nor joyous. To be honest, I don't really like changing songs after I've written them because that's how they simply came out. As corny as it may sound, I don't choose the song, the songs truly choose me. I need to just write all my emotions down on paper so I can get this tight, twisted feeling off of my chest.

Songwriting has always been an escape for me, and when it started to feel like a job in my later years of Insieme, it started to become toxic. Samantha would constantly tell me to change my lyrics, and I would always worry about people's expectations of our new album, so I feel like my songs never came out as good as they could have been. I never had enough time to just perfect it or tweak it, or let it naturally flow out of me because I was always on a deadline. And do you think I ever got any help from the boys? No.

I shake my head as I put on my "Scarecrow" CD. I love using my CD player because I can listen to music without looking at my phone and getting distracted or having my heart sink from a notification that I don't want to see.

I tap my foot along with the beat as I stare at my blank page, wondering what I could write about. Self-discovery is kind of out of the question because I don't really know who I am anymore. A love song is too sensitive right now because I am feeling nothing close to happiness from relationships. Maybe I could talk about the complicatedness of relationships and how communication can resolve a lot of problems, but it would be pretty ironic of me.

I start to look back on my life and all the people I've hurt. Of course, I always think about how bad I've hurt my friends and family, but what about my fans? I think I'm well past due for a formal apology to my fans who did nothing but support me, only for me to disappoint them and then disappear.

As words start to spill out, I think the same thought I had when I wrote "I Was Wrong": *this could work.*

You know me, I'm never satisfied
Don't blame me, we all got pride.
Money, booze, and awards,
I kept needing those rewards.
Blame it on others is all I did
'Till I went completely off the grid.
You see, I've been working day in and day out
To make things right, but it isn't enough without a doubt.
Trying to get better,
When will it ever be enough?
The old me- trying my best to forget her
Seems like my life is always in the rough.

"Yes!" I exclaim out loud, proud that I came up with simple lyrics that can go with a soft piano melody.

Do I ever cross your mind?
Even when I've been gone all this time

And running wild?

But at least self-isolation isn't a crime.

But can sorry cover the costs

Of all the time we've lost?

I miss you like crazy and I apologize.

See there's more to life I've come to realize.

Can't change the past, just gotta make a
better me that lasts.

Please just take me back.

I love the song I've just come up with because for me, I'm talking directly and personally to the fans, but it's also something that I think is applicable to anyone's situation. If someone is going through a break up, they can relate to this song. Or if they randomly stopped talking to all their friends because they're mental health has started to slowly decrease and they don't know how to ask for help, they can relate to this song.

Now I just need to come up with a title, and head down to the music store to buy myself a keyboard.

Chapter 33

Tony

By the time I get to Giovanna's room, I'm sweating buckets because the Uber driver had the heat cranked up to full blast. Maybe he was menopausal, I don't know, but all I know is that the mixture of alcohol in my system and being in that car has caused me to feel extremely nauseous.

I knock on her door and patiently wait for her to answer. I have to slouch against the door just because of how exhausted I am. I forgot how drowsy scotch makes me.

"Giovanna, please open up, it's me," I say, having a hard time talking without dry heaving. I know for a fact she's in there, and I'm honestly going to be pissed if I paid 75 dollars for an Uber, just for her to not open this door. I knock again, but there's still now answer.

I sit on the floor, tucking my knees into my chest as I wait for Giovanna to get back. I don't even know why I'm here, or why I thought it would be a good idea know to love her.

Wow. I'm really drunk.

I can barely even get my thoughts straight.

I'm trying to say that I don't know what to do with my life. It feels like Insieme finally had their last breaking point, and whatever little flicker of hope was left of a reunion is now dwindled out.

Do I love my job now? Sure, but it's not touring the world with my two best friends, and I don't know if I'll ever be able to say goodbye to that lifestyle.

I'm not sure if I came here to tell Giovanna that I don't want to talk to her or Luca ever again, or if I came to beg her to help me out. I have so many emotions swirling around in my brain that I just need someone to ground me for a second. Plus, she owes me that much, since I'm constantly listening to her rant about her issues. I just know what to do.

I feel lost.

I *am* lost.

Do you know how hard it is to feel alienated every damn day of your life? Because I feel it every

single day, and I'm sick of it. It's times like these-
when even my best friend points out how
embarrassingly single I am- that I wish I could be
somebody, *anybody* else.

Sometimes I don't want to be Tony from
Insieme. I just want to be Tony, simple and smart
like I used to be. It's hard when I start thinking that
way because then those thoughts just follow with
this feeling of guilt. I feel guilty that I would ever
want to change my life because I sound so
privileged and it makes me seem ungrateful for all
the opportunities I've had.

I just want Giovanna to come here so I can
actually say these thoughts out loud. I've heard that
when you're feeling down or angry or whatever,
you're supposed to journal, write, or talk it out of
your system. That way, it's off of your chest and
you feel a little lighter. But how can I start now
when I've been told to compress who I am and my
feelings for all 25 years of my life?

Let alone the fact that I couldn't even be in a
relationship with a man for four years of my life,

but a man hasn't even looked at me romantically once in my life. If there's one thing about me, it's that I am the king of the friendzone. Every time I think that maybe a friend of mine feels the same about me, they come and hit me with the: "Hey, I know we're hanging out soon, but I just want to make it clear that this isn't a date". That leads me to cry my little sad heart out for days, wondering what's wrong with me.

Because why am I not enough? What could possibly be so bad about me that completely grosses everyone out? My uneven features and non-symmetrical face? Or perhaps it has nothing to do with my looks at all and everything to do with my personality. Maybe I'm too weird, too loud, and just too much for anyone to want to spend the rest of their life with me.

I really underestimated the percentage of alcohol in that scotch. However, these "drunk" thoughts are the same one's I've had for years, even when I'm sober. I've been silenced by even my closest friends because they're too selfish to even ask how I'm doing.

Well, there's going to be none of that anymore, if Giovanna ever gets back to her room.

Chapter 34

Giovanna

I didn't consider how large keyboards are, and I don't want to remember how I nearly choked when I saw that the cheapest one was $175, but I bought it anyway. I figured it'd be one of those investments that'd be worth it.

When I walk up to my door, I'm greeted by a strange sight to say the least. "Tony?" I ask, ducking down to make sure it's him. "What are you doing here?"

He looks up at me and I can already tell that he's drunk. Not only have I seen him drunk multiple times, but I've seen that same relaxed gaze staring back at me when I look in the mirror. He points his finger at my keyboard. "What's that?"

I look at my Yamaha keyboard and then back at him. "I need it for something."

"For what?"

"A project I'm working on."

"You know what Luca said to me before I got here?" he asks, changing the subject right away, as if he has no recollection of the conversation we were just having. "He told me that I'm going to be single for the rest of my life, basically," he says, not waiting for me to answer.

"Come inside, T," I say, punching in my code and opening the door. I walk in and place my keyboard on the bed and go back out to help Tony to his feet. "How long have you been out here?" What is it with the boys never telling me when they're planning to come over?

He shrugs his shoulders. "Long enough to realize that I'm officially going through my mid-life crisis."

"Explain to me what happened, Tony."

And so, he tells me every little detail, losing track of the topic multiple times as he explains how Luca and him got into an argument. It seems to me like Luca has an issue with everyone, but I know that I'm- as usual- the root of the issue here.

"Tony, I am so sorry he said that to you. I know how hard it is, but he was just mad at me and not you-"

"No, you don't!" he yells suddenly, causing me to jerk my hand off his shoulder. "You don't understand me, Giovanna. You never will because you're not in my shoes and you have no idea what it's like to live my life in constant fear. In constant *judgment*."

I mean, what can I say to that? He's right and there's nothing I can say at this point to comfort him. I know probably better than anybody else that ranting when you're drunk is the most freeing thing one can do. I would also be lying if I said my eyes aren't darting around rapidly, looking to get my hands on even a single drop of alcohol.

"It hurts because I've been with him through thick and thin, and then he goes and says that crap to me? What did I do to deserve it? At the end of the day, I'm not the reason Insieme broke up, you are, Giovanna, and so is Luca. So, I don't know why he's so mad at me." His words punch me right in the gut, but I can't say that he's wrong.

"Maybe he just needed someone to yell at and you just so happened to be the only person who was there," I suggest, knowing that I've had my fair share of unnecessary snaps at innocent people.

"I don't know exactly what to do here, Gia. Am I just supposed to forget every single memory I have with Insieme? Pretend like I'm not a singer? Go on and live my day bussing tables for ungrateful customers who think they're above people in hospitality? I'm sick of it! I wanted Insieme to get back together, and when you actually went to a meeting, I thought that things were turning around, but I can't wrap my head around the fact that two toddlers are ruining my life."

"Tony, I don't know what to tell you. Maybe Insieme will get back together, but right now, you need to go to bed and sober up." Usually, this conversation is totally flipped. I've never, *ever* been the one to tell someone to go to bed and sober up; this is all so new to me, and I'm not sure I'm doing a good job.

My phone buzzes in my pocket and when I look at it, I see that my sobriety tracker is telling me that I've hit my one-day sobriety mark.

"Who's that?" he asks, his eyes moving a hundred miles an hour.

"I'm one day sober," I say, smiling and looking down at my phone as I send a text over to Danny and share the news with him.

"Oh my gosh," he whispers, slouching to the ground. "I'm so sorry. I'm so sorry, Giovanna."

"For what?" I ask, putting my phone back down.

"I didn't even think of how triggering it would be for me to show up plastered in your room. I just wanted to talk to you and I let my emotions get the best of me. I'm so sorry that I came here in the first place… but that doesn't mean I don't mean what I said. I think you're an asshole still."

He's so drunk right now and I can barely understand him. I was supposed to start working on the song and putting some music to the lyrics that I wrote. Now I have to decide between Tony and the song, and it's breaking my heart. "It's okay, T," I say, trying to see if he's going to speak more, but he doesn't. "Why don't you just crash here tonight?" I suggest.

This is now how my night was supposed to go at all, but when a friend is knocking- no, when *family* is calling- you never shut the door.

"You look like you had something else in mind," he states, nodding his head at the keyboard lying in the room.

I shrug my shoulders. "I owe you at least one night after all the times you've had to carry me home."

He nods his head, but doesn't say anything more. He just simply crawls into bed and instantly closes his eyes as soon as his head hits my pillow.

"Tony?" I ask.

Silence.

I shake my head as I look at my keyboard. *What a crazy life.*

Chapter 35

Luca

I'm about to head out to work when Tony comes trudging into our flat. He stares at me blankly and I look back, knowing I should apologize and tell him I was out of line. Somehow, though, the words get all clumped in my throat and I know that if I open my mouth, I will cry.

"Hey," I barely say, focusing on pouring my coffee into a thermos.

"Hey," he replies, walking in as if everything is normal.

"Want some coffee?" I offer.

"Yes, please."

I grab a mug for him and fill it, adding just one teaspoon of sugar. "Tony, I'm really-"

"It's okay," he cuts me off. "I don't want to talk about it."

I stare at him as I give him his coffee. "Okay, well, I wanted to just say that I'm truly sorry for how I acted. At least let me apologize."

"There's nothing to apologize for."

"I'm sorry, Tony, I didn't mean what I said at all."

When I act like that- when I let my emotions get the best of me- it embarrasses me. It reminds me of Vince, and I hate the fact that I'm related to him. I know where Vince and I get our temper from, and I'm saddened to admit that we act like our grandfather when we snap. It's as though we dissociate and almost become crazy to the point where nothing can calm us down and take us back to reality. The fact that I act exactly like the men in my life who I never wanted to become not only bruises my pride, but it harms those closest to me.

"I know," he clips. "I would just appreciate it if you didn't take your anger out in such an ignorant way next time."

He's exactly right, when I'm angry, I become incredibly ignorant that I want to punch myself. I can't explain it to you, and I wish it was just as easy as recognizing that I'm getting angry and taking a few deep breaths to calm down.

However, craziness isn't that easily tamed. I almost turn manic, unrecognizable.

"You better head out before you're late," he tells me, urging me out as subtly as possible. I nod my head and walk out, heading out to another hard day's worth of work.

My father- may every good thing in this universe come to him- did not provide my brother's and I a prosperous lifestyle by sitting on the couch all day. He got up in the early hours of the morning when most of the world was still fast asleep, and performed back-breaking work. He worked his way to the top in the construction industry so he could eventually become self-employed, and I will never be half the man he is.

For that, he is completely different from my grandfather. As far as I'm concerned, he's as good as dead to me, and I wish Lorenzo would recognize that too. Enzo's too young to remember all of the horrible things he put our family through, and in fact, Lorenzo is the only Fonzo still in contact with him. Lorenzo and I have budded heads on the situation multiple times, but we're able to respect each other's decisions when it comes to our own relationship with our grandfather.

Speaking of my younger and favorite brother, I haven't heard from him in a while. When he found out that Insieme was over, it absolutely crushed him. I know he's a grown man now, but he'll always be that little kid to me and he's always going to be a priority. It crushed me, *destroyed* me, when he told me how disappointed he was that the three of us couldn't figure out our careers. He's always thought highly of Gia, even though sometimes he shouldn't, and it pains me every day that I can't give him the news he's always looking for when it comes to Giovanna and I's relationship.

It seems as though everyone wants the two of us to get back together. My mother would be over the moon that Gia's family would be her in-laws, my father loves Giovanna like his own daughter, and Lorenzo has been waiting for the day to officially call Giovanna his sister-in-law for years. However, I shouldn't say that everyone would be thrilled because Vince despises her. He's constantly telling me that I'm a disgrace for chasing after her dreams and leaving our family behind, as if he didn't move away for school and left me to watch over Lorenzo. He can't stand the fact that I gave up football, but I didn't even have a scholarship offer to accept when the record deal was on the table, so I'm not too sure why he's always had a bee in his bonnet about Giovanna and Insieme in general.

As I'm driving to the job site, I start to think about my relationship and where it's gone wrong. You know, I've always heard people talk about love at first sight, but to be completely honest with you, I've never thought it was true. It seems as though everything changed when I met Giovanna. Even before Insieme started, she caught my eye. I can't exactly blame myself for being a shy, awkward teenager, but I think we definitely would have hit it off sooner if I had just gotten over myself and asked her to dance.

As time went on, things got complicated between us, and it seems like everyone sees how good we are together more than Giovanna and I do sometimes. Even the press labeled us as the world's best couple, and now they're wondering if we're even still together. When the odd article here or there shows up on my phone about the writer's conspiracies on our relationship, I can't help but shake my head because it's really none of their business. We have a hard time figuring things out on our own as it is, we don't need people to give us their unnecessary opinions.

Especially now that Danny is in the picture and I can't help all the insecure feelings that have returned to me. Can you blame me, though? I mean, after our first kiss, Giovanna acted as though she didn't remember anything. Do you have any idea how much that hurt me? How unwanted and unloved that made me feel? Just for her to run off and post pictures with Danny on her Instagram two weeks after the fact, and I was just supposed to be confident in myself and act like nothing happened?

That's the thing with Giovanna: she makes me feel like I'm competing. When you're in love, you should feel like a champion. You shouldn't feel like you're still running the marathon after you've received the gold medal. With Giovanna, it feels like I'm not only sprinting another hundred meters after the finish line, but I'm also jumping through fifty hurdles to get to her.

She's built up such a wall, and whether that's because of her past experiences or not, it makes me feel as though I'm never going to be good enough for her. As though she's always going to be searching for the next best man to come along and sweep her off her feet. Especially after I dropped everything to drive her to the Alcoholics Anonymous meeting, only for her to turn all her attention to Danny and not so much as say thank you to me.

When I roll onto the job site, I'm greeted by my dad wearing a huge smile on his face. "Luca! How's it going?"

"Hey, Pa," I respond, trying my best to return his smile.

"Everything okay?"

I look at him, contemplating if I should be the strong man he raised and nod my head, or break down and give him a hug that I so desperately need right now.

Somehow, I end up doing a mix of both. I nod my head as tears stream down my cheeks. "Luca, what's wrong?" he asks with a puzzled expression on his face.

"My life, Pa, it's just so complicated," I whisper, trying not to make that big of a deal.

He gives my shoulder a slap and forces me to look into his eyes. "Luca, I worked my whole life to make sure you had a great life. I bust my ass every day to put food on the table, but I couldn't prepare you for the kind of career you chose, son."

"What do you mean?" I ask, wiping my eyes with the heels of my hand.

"I've been reading articles, I've been hearing things here and there, and I know what you've been doing for Giovanna recently. Luca, I know you love her and you've done nothing but show that, so don't be an idiot and let that go to waste."

"I've been trying to save us, Pa, I really have," I explain.

He shakes his head, looking at me with those old eyes. "No, you haven't. Luca, you're my son, and I love you, but I didn't raise you to be like this. The two of you are too stubborn to put your pride and ego aside and communicate with each other, and that is not the man that I raised you to be. You have to go fight for her, because I know she's your person, your soulmate."

I look up at him, barely able to see through my tears and I can't help the smile that breaks onto my face. "Women, hey, Pa?"

He shakes his head and sighs. "Yep. But men aren't such a treat either."

That much is true, and if there's one thing I can't lose in my life again, it's that damn woman.

Chapter 36

Giovanna

3:04 AM is the time my phone is telling me. I've watched this video hundreds of times, listening to how my voice sounds. How the lyrics flow with the soft, weeping melancholy of a melody I came up with on my keyboard. Oh, how I've missed music.

Sure, Nancy has been great to deal with and I'm seeing her tomorrow, but sometimes, music is the only therapy that can cure the heart and soul.

I'm honestly scared of people who don't have music playing all day, every day. I don't care if it's on my phone or if it's my CD player spinning, I need music to fill the silence because it's like injecting pure joy into my veins.

I play the video again, listening to how perfect my pitch is. I also notice how my hair is bouncing loosely around my shoulders with every key I press and how in control I look. Amidst all the drama, I forgot that I was a born singer.

I know I've said it before, but this time I mean it when I say that my life is back on the right track. I've been sober for one week, the longest I've ever been able to stay sober, and I've got a great support system with my Alcoholics Anonymous group and Danny. So much so that I asked Willow to be my sponsor when we went for coffee yesterday, and she rejoiced and said yes. It feels like I'm finally able to live my life without having to constantly drink, and although it's been a tough journey, I'm starting to see how nice the rewards are. I also can't help but notice the little bit of weight I've dropped since cutting alcohol out, and how I've made great friends who understand me in A.A.

The only thing that's missing in my life right now are my family and music. I owe it to my family, especially Antonio, to reach out, but seeing as though it is three in the morning, I'm not going to bother him at this hour. Tomorrow, I pledge to myself that I will give him a call.

But you know what I can do right now? I can get music back into my life. I can give the fans what they've been asking for since June 13th. I can gain them back if I just hit the upload button right now. They'll be extremely excited to see that I'm back, though I'm not sure how they'll react to the fact that it's just me in the video.

What if they hate it and there ends up being more thumbs down than thumbs up? Or if they tell me I'm nothing without the boys? Or if they think the lyrics are too sad, too sappy?

My phone starts to shake in my hands because of my nerves. All the anxiety I had when I was 16 is running through my mind as I seriously consider if I should or shouldn't hit the red button. I take a deep breath and squeeze my eyes shut.

I can do this.

I can show the world I still love them and can only hope that they still love me. At this point, it's not about doing it for the glory, it's about getting my life back, and my life is simply music.

I tap the upload button.

20% complete.

I shouldn't have done that.

45% complete.

I should have talked to the boys before doing this.

79% complete.

Is someone knocking on my door, or is that my heart pounding?

93% complete.

Cancel. Cancel. Cancel.

100% complete.

I throw my phone across the room, unsure if I just made the best or worst decision of my life.

Chapter 37

Luca

I hear Tony choke on his snore as I walk into his room.

"What time is it?" he asks, his voice groggy from sleep.

"Tony, you gotta see this right now." I turn the lights on, causing him to cringe from the sudden brightness.

"What the…" he trails off as I play him the video. "Is that…?" He rubs his eyes, as if he can't believe what he's seeing.

"Yup." I can't believe it myself. At first, I thought surely that this was all a dream and not real life, a hallucination. But no. No, the thousands of messages flooding my phone reminded me that this is very much real.

I watch the video again, noticing the view count go up to just over one million views now. She posted the video five hours ago.

Tony looks up at me with big eyes once the video is over. "That was beautiful." I have to agree, it truly was. I don't know who that song is dedicated to, but all I know is that the fans seemed to have loved it. I scroll through the thousands of comments and notice how much love she is receiving from strangers, and it makes my heart swell.

"I wasn't expecting this," I admit.

He snickers. "Ain't that the truth."

"We have to call her, don't you think?"

He shakes his head. "Screw that, tell her to come over here."

So, I do. I send her a text and she tells me she's going to be here in twenty minutes. I get up and pace because I've been hanging out with Tony too much and have picked up his nervous habits.

Lorenzo's name pops up and my phone starts buzzing and Tony tells me to pick up the call immediately.

"Hello," I say.

"Are you seeing this?" he asks, half excited, half in denial.

"Yep."

"Did you know she was going to do this?"

"No," Tony and I blurt at the same time.

He lets out a laugh on the other line. "You guys, this is huge. It's blowing up! This shows that you guys could drop a song right now and absolutely shatter the charts," he gushes.

"I know." It makes my heart do somersaults in my chest, but nothing is set in stone until Giovanna walks through that door.

"Look, I got a shift to head to, but I'm expecting updates," Lorenzo says, ending the call before Tony and I even have a chance to say goodbye to him.

And then there's a small, barely noticeable knock on the door.

"How much do you think she tipped the taxi driver to speed?" Tony mutters under his breath as he opens the door.

"I'm so sorry, I should have told you guys I was planning on uploading this song," she spits out as soon as she sees us, as if we are going to be mad at her for doing something by herself.

"Giovanna-" I start, but the lady is too lost in her own world to shut her mouth.

"I didn't even plan on posting the video. I just sort of had this crisis and the lyrics just spawned out of me and so I bought this keyboard. I really didn't have the money for the keyboard, but I got it anyways, and I thought it would be a waste if I didn't share the song, so I-"

"Giovanna, stop."

"Luca, please, don't be mad."

"I'm not mad at you, I'm actually…"

But how do I feel? I don't know. I've barely had time to process what exactly is happening here and what this means for my own career.

"You're actually what?" she asks, sucking in a breath.

I look at the woman I love and realize just how far she's come as my father's words play through my mind. To say she's completely turned her life around would be an understatement. She went from average, to high, to extremely low, to everything in between, and now she's what I've always thought she needed to be: stable.

"I'm actually proud of you," I hush, stepping closer to her. We hold eye contact, neither of us daring to speak, knowing words would just complicate things. Her cheeks turn completely red as she twists her body closer to mine. For a moment, I think time has stopped at this perfect moment.

Until my phone starts ringing. I pull it out of my back as Gia lets out a nervous chuckle and takes a step back, smiling at Tony who is too stunned to speak.

I look up at the two of them with huge eyes. "You guys, I don't know if I should take this call."

"Who is it?" Tony asks.

I blink a few times to ensure that I'm not making this up. "Samantha."

Tony freezes with his jaw on the floor and my thumb is hovering over the decline button.

"Give me the phone," Giovanna peeps, extending out her hand. I know this is crushing her inside, and I can't imagine how much anger she's feeling right now. Somehow, some way, she's keeping it better than Tony and I can.

"Hello," she answers the phone with such confidence.

"Oh, I must have the wrong number." I hear through the muffled speaker.

"This is Luca's phone."

"Put it on speaker," Tony whispers, swatting at Giovanna's arm until she does.

"We're all here," Giovanna informs her. I've never seen Giovanna remain so calm before.

"Oh. Well, that's perfect. How are you all doing?" she asks, as if she didn't ruin all of our lives.

"What do you want, Samantha?" Giovanna asks coldly, showing that she couldn't be bothered.

She clears her throat. "Reen has noticed how much Giovanna's recent video has blown up, and we see all the demands for Insieme to get back together."

Giovanna looks at me, and I can tell her wall is crumbling down. She never wanted to speak to Samantha ever again, and this is tough for her, so I take over.

"People have been asking us to get back together for months," I point out, getting nods back from Gia and Tony.

"Well, we couldn't take you guys back because Giovanna was too much of a loose cannon," she counters. "However, seeing as though people love your music, I want to offer you a deal."

Giovanna is shaking her head rapidly at me, but it's Tony who takes over the conversation now. "What kind of deal?" he inquires, sending Giovanna's eyes popping right out of their sockets.

"Four years, $65,000 per year, with the condition that you release an album every *two* years."

Giovanna shuts her eyes. "We'll have to give you a call back," she says against every bone in her body. She hangs up before the conversation can carry on.

Giovanna hands my phone back and pulls her buzzing phone out. "Oh my gosh!" she exclaims, jumping into me and wrapping her legs around my waist, nearly knocking me over.

"What?" Tony asks with a disgusted look on his face. "You want to go back to Reen?"

"No! Gosh, no! My brother texted me telling me that he's sorry and that he loves me. I bet you saw my video," she shrieks with excitement.

I spring her around and laugh with her. "That's amazing, Giovanna."

We stay wrapped in each other until she climbs down and straightens out her clothes. "I have a therapy appointment, and I think the three of us should consider if we want to take the offer or not. How about I come back after my appointment?"

"Sounds good, want a ride?" Tony offers, but she shakes her head.

She turns to head out. "I'll be back."

"Giovanna, wait," I blurt, stopping her dead in her tracks. "We really are proud of you."

She breaks out into a genuine, beaming smile. "Thank you."

Just by the way she carries herself as she walks out the door, I can tell that she's proud of herself, too.

Chapter 38

Giovanna

"So, she offered you a contract," Nancy says with a smile, "and you accepted it?"

"No, not yet. After my appointment, I'm going back to see the boys and we're going to call her with our final decision," I explain.

She throws her head back back with a sigh. "I see."

I smile. "I'm so glad people love my video. I was nervous they were going to hate the song."

"See, sometimes we hurt ourselves by overthinking things that haven't even happened yet."

"Believe me, I know." There's no need for her to lecture me on overthinking.

"What do you think you're going to do with the deal?"

I bury my face in my hands. "Please don't ask me, please just give me the answer," I say with a laugh. I'm only half joking, of course.

"No, no, you need to make this decision yourself. You need to do what you think is best for you and what you think you can handle right now. That's the main reason why I ask you so many questions, rather than giving you my advice as to what you should do. My job is to not give you the answer, my job is to listen to you and allow you to come to your own conclusion by yourself." She looks at me with a proud smile on her face, as if she can tell a lightbulb has just gone off above my head.

"I know. It's just all happening so fast, yet I don't want it to stop. I forgot how good it feels to get love from hundreds and thousands of strangers."

She cocks her head to the side." And what about your family? Have they seen the video?"

"Yes! Antonio actually texted me and we've cleared out the bad blood between us over the phone. I'm going out to dinner with my family next weekend, I believe, actually."

"That's fantastic," she comments.

"I just didn't think I had it in me. You know when you're stuck in such a low part of your life that you don't think you can ever bounce back?"

She nods her head slowly. "But you have been able to get better. You. Not Luca, not Tony, not your family, not the fans, and not even me. It was you who picked yourself up and dusted yourself off."

She's making my ego grow by the moment, but I don't mind at all because I know she's one hundred percent right.

"I don't know what I'm going to do honestly, but all I know is that writing the song has been a nice distraction from drinking. Did I tell you that I'm eight days sober?"

She claps her hands excitedly. "Great! I'm glad music is an escape for you and takes your mind off of things." There's something in her eyes that is telling me there is much more she wants to say.

"What?"

"What?" she fires back with a small smirk.

I roll my eyes. "Say that thought out loud."

She closes her notebook and leans her elbows on her knees like I've seen her do a hundred times before. "Remember when you were telling me about the first meeting you went to?" I nod my head. "That man, I can't remember his name."

"Thomas?" I ask.

"Right! He was talking about how his drinking was a blessing in disguise."

"I know."

"And do you think you've been able to see if that relates to you?"

I shake my head. "Now that I'm alcohol free- hopefully, for a long time- I honestly couldn't tell you."

She sets her lips in a firm line, something I've never seen her do before. "I know what it is."

"Tell me," I demand, practically jumping out of my seat.

"No, you need to recognize it yourself."

"Please, just tell me," I beg.

She looks down at her watch. "Looks like that's all the time we have for today's session. I'm seeing you in a week, and I have faith you will have an answer for me."

"You can't just kick me out!" My voice is irritably high-pitched, but I want to know the blessing in disguise.

"Goodbye, Giovanna, I have to see another patient now."

So, Nancy, for the first time ever, kicks me out of her office. Yet again, I'm left with only questions and no answers. However, it's a good thing I have a whole train ride to think about it before I see the boys.

Chapter 39

Giovanna

When I get back to their place, the boys are busy talking amongst themselves. They're talking about how my video has ten million views now and continues to break the news, and how they can't believe we can get our record deal back.

"This is what we've been waiting for," Luca says, bouncing off the walls. "We lost it, but fate brought it back to us."

I whip out my phone, getting hundreds of messages from old friends. I get texts from Jana, Kassie, and even Mary to congratulate me on such a beautiful song. Although Mary and I haven't made up and I don't think we ever will go back to how things were, I'm glad that we're mutual enough to respect each other now.

"I say we take the deal," he suggests. "What do you guys think?" Luca honestly looks like a kid in a candy shop, and it's almost enough to make me want to say yes right away, but Tony starts talking before I have the chance.

"Sure, Giovanna has changed and is sober, but what about them? Don't get me wrong, I would love to go back on tour, but does it have to be with Reen? Who's to say they've changed? Are they more accepting of who I am? What if you and Giovanna want to get married, will they allow that? And notice how they didn't help us when we fell apart? They only want us at our highs and not our lows, and that pisses me right off."

There it is.

That's what Nancy was talking about.

The boys are not necessarily arguing, but they're getting passionate about what decision to make, but I've tuned them out at this point. My ear has started to ring and suddenly I am a thousand degrees. I can feel my clothes sticking to me and feel the need to sit down immediately before I faint. Thankful, the boys are too lost in their conversation to notice my panic attack, allowing me some time alone with my thoughts.

My blessing in disguise when it comes to drinking actually does exist. Although my drinking problem was out of control and it's still extremely fragile, and yes, I am aware that I have a long way to go when it comes to sobriety, it saved me just like it saved Thomas from his marriage.

My drinking saved me from Reen.

It cost me the deal, but it let me get out of that toxic management environment. It allowed me to be free of those people treating me like a puppet and controlling everything I ever did.

That's my blessing in disguise Nancy was trying to tell me about.

"No," I whisper.

"What was that, *amore*?" Luca asks, placing his hand on my knee.

"No. I'm not accepting that offer."

Tony nods his head. "It's two against one, we need to call her and let her know our decision."

"I'm not saying no to Insieme breaking up forever, but I'm saying no to Reen. We got out of that toxic management, albeit a bit horrendously, and I will not put us back there. We can find another record label that would be more than happy to have us, but we are not going back to Reen. End of discussion."

Tony and Luca stare at each other, having a conversation with their eyes, but I know I have them convinced. Before I know it, Luca is calling Samantha back.

She picks up on the first ring. "So? Are you guys going to take the deal?"

"No," I say, speaking for all of us.

Look at us, going full circle. From being teens impulsively agreeing to a toxic workplace on speaker phone, to (somewhat) mature adults standing our ground on speaker phone with the same person years later.

"No?" she sneers. "You're joking, right?"

"No, we are declining the offer," I repeat, a bit more confidently this time.

"Why?"

"Let's just put it this way: Insieme is going to come back and we are going to release another album. However, we will never, ever sign with Reen again. In fact, I wish Reen would shut its doors right now because the way you treat your customers is terrifying. To say you're toxic would be an understatement. Let alone that, it's time for Insieme to move on, so we are not going to take the offer."

I hang up and wipe my sweaty palms on my pants. I stare at Luca and Tony who look like they are two deer in the headlights.

"What now?" Luca asks.

I smile at him. "Three things: let's go for dinner, write some songs, and then go searching for a new record label."

Tony beams at me. "Giovanna Rossi, I'm so glad you're back."

"It's good to be back together. I love you guys," I say.

Luca squeezes my hand. "We love you, too."

"Does this mean you two are finally back together without any drama?" Tony asks, half joking, half serious.

Luca squeezes my hand again, reassuring me that we are great and we will get through everything together like we always have before.

"That's all in the past," I begin, ready to give the speech they always leave up to me. "All the toxic, petty, and dramatic behavior is in the past. We lost sight of our roots when we were a Grammy Award Winning trio, and I'm going to do everything in my power to make sure that doesn't happen again.

"Now, perhaps we may not get a deal, but I'm pretty damn sure any label would be stupid to decline us." That makes the boys laugh and it makes my heart swell. "Look, we all fall off the wagon here or there, but let's just look forward to tomorrow, live in the moment, and remember the past. Right now, it's time for Insieme to start fresh."

Chapter 40

Giovanna

"Today, I am five months sober," I declare to everyone in the Alcoholics Anonymous meeting. As I catch Danny's gleaming and proud eyes, I can't help but smile. He volunteered me to do another testimony, something I haven't done since my first meeting, and after all he's done for me, I couldn't say no. I receive a few claps from people, especially Willow.

"For those of you who don't know me, my name is Giovanna Rossi, and I'm a singer with Insieme. I signed a record deal when I was 16, and I was tremendously unprepared for the dark side of Hollywood. Obviously, I turned to drinking to take away the pain. To make a long story short, alcohol was my remedy for a lost soul. I ended up missing a huge deadline because I was too busy drinking myself to death.

"It seemed as though I had lost everything from drinking. I lost my boyfriend, my best friend, my family, and my career. Drinking turned me into a monster." I get a few nods as people relate to every word that comes out of my mouth. I can't help but notice the shaking of my hand, and I try to take a few deep breaths as I carry on.

"When I moved back home, I started seeing a therapist. One tragic event led to another, and I ended up in a meeting here. What stood out to me the most was my response to my therapist when she asked me what my goal was. She wanted to know what I wanted to feel like after my session with her, and I simply told her that I wanted to be content.

"Throughout my entire life, I've always searched for more. Every time I had something great, it never seemed to be enough for me, and I wanted that to stop. That feeling of always longing for more played a huge factor in my drinking as well, because the more unhappy I was, the more I drank. However, as I started coming to A.A. meetings regularly, made amends with those who I had hurt, and started to dive into the journey of self-care, I became more and more content with my life with every day that passed."

I take another deep breath. "I ended up getting back together with Insieme, and we are now set to move to New York in two months because we signed with a label out there. I would be lying to you if I wasn't nervous. These meetings and therapy have become part of my daily routine, and I had just repaired my relationship with my family, so I don't want to mess everything up. I've stayed up many nights thinking about whether or not I should go."

Danny clears his throat. "And what have you decided?" he asks softly.

I nod my head. "I'm going to go. Ultimately, when I look back on the past two years of my life, I can see how much I've grown for the better. If for some reason I trip and fall again, I know that I can pull myself back up because I have done so before."

I look around and see every single set of eyes on me, and I can see how they're all full of hope and compassion. "I don't think you'll fall, Giovanna," Danny says nicely.

I hang my head for a moment before I look into his eyes. "I don't see how I could either."

This is the fresh start I need, and I have a feeling this album is going to be the best. Since being sober, my mind has been peaceful. There is no longer this constant thunderstorm roaring in my mind twenty-four hours for seven days a week, and I feel balanced.

Luca and I have decided to get back together, but we aren't engaged yet because we need to learn from our mistakes and take things slower this time around. Tony and I are stronger than ever, and I can say the exact same thing about my family and other friends.

I've done a lot of wrong in my life, but music still remains. I still remain.

I am still a girl with the dream, but this is now the next chapter in my life.

Acknowledgements

First and foremost, I would like to send a ginormous thank you to my family. You have constantly supported me throughout this entire process, and I could not have published three books without you. Mom, thank you for listening to all my book ideas. Dad, thank you for reasoning with me and talking me through everything. Joseph, thank you for making me laugh when I get stressed about these books. And of course, to my dog Remy, thank you for cuddling next to me whenever I sit down to type.

I would also like to give a special thank you to my book cover designer Isabella Alvarez Lalama. Shoutout to you for always knowing exactly what I need, and I don't know how you were able to pull off such an amazing cover with my horrible communication skills.

To my fans and supporters, I would not have been able to publish three books before I graduated high school without you. I want you to know that I see all your comments and reviews that are filled with constant support, and I am overwhelmed by them in the best way possible. Thank you for showing continual love and support for me.

To all of my friends, well, I don't even know where to begin. Specifically, you, Ryan. You have been with me through all of my crazy emotions during this publishing process. Not only have you been a constant source of happiness and encouragement, but you constantly bring a smile to my face and have shown me the true meaning of friendship.

To my extended family, thank you for showing me how proud you are. Every time I write, I write for you.

Well, it's been a hell of a ride for Giovanna, and thank you for seeing her through until the end.

Manufactured by Amazon.ca
Bolton, ON

34592926R00187